C0-APM-811

ESCAPING FROM FOREVER

Battle Born MC- Reno

Book Five

BY

Scarlett Black

Escaping from Forever
Copyright © 2019 By Scarlett Black
All rights reserved.

No part of this publication may be used or reproduced in any manner whatsoever, including but not limited to being stored in a retrieval system or transmitted in any form or by any means electronical, mechanical, photocopying, recording or otherwise, without the written permission of the author.

This book is a work of fiction. Names, characters, groups, businesses, and incidents either are the product of the author's imagination or are used fictitiously. Any resemblance to actual places or persons, living or dead, is entirely coincidental.

Cover Art by Opium House Creatives

WARNING: This book contains sexual situations and VERY adult themes. Recommended for 18 and above.

ESCAPING FROM FOREVER

Some wars are won by sacrificing the Queen.

Life demanded Katherine become stronger than the men around her, all of whom were willing to use her as a pawn in their deceptive games. They robbed her of her will and silenced her voice until she reached her breaking point and broke free. It would be over her dead body before she would ever allow herself to be dragged back into that toxic existence.

Tank thought he was living his best life. What more could he want than stacks of cash and an endless supply of women? One night with Kat is all it takes to introduce him to the passionate connection he's been missing, and leave him aching for more.

But when Kat's past catches up with her, it comes with the startlingly revelation of just how far the cartel will go to destroy the MC. Desperate not to return to the life she left behind, Kat concocts a dangerous plan with fatal risks. Can Tank get there in time to stop her?

Or will their relationship be yet another casualty in the brewing war?

PART ONE

The beginning tale of Tank & Kat, a love found in the dark

CHAPTER 1

Tank

Las Vegas

The beer bottle turns round and round in my hands while I sit and listen to the radio station play the top ten hits of the 90's. My mind is stuck on replay, and I stare into the dark glass. The memories come back to the front of my mind, along with the anger of what happened six months ago.

Ava jumps up and down in the airport, waiting for me over by the baggage claim as I come down the escalator. Both of us flew back in from the holiday vacation at the same time. Her long blonde hair is pulled back into a ponytail, and her lean legs flex with every jump. I slide my headphones off, leaving them around my neck, and turn my CD player off, then tuck it inside the front pocket of my University of Las Vegas hoodie.

As soon as I reach the floor, she has her lips plastered to mine. It's a dirty 'I'm fucking your mouth because my dick hasn't been used since I left Nevada for Christmas, and I would like nothing more than to cram my dick down your throat' *kind of kiss. I'm hard, and it's painful in these jeans.*

I hear a mother clearing her throat as she's pushing her kids along, clearly disgusted with my hand that's full of Ava's fuckin' fine, cheerleader ass. A man accidently hits us from behind and Ava laughs.

"How was Christmas break with your parents?" she asks tentatively while we walk over to collect my bag.

"Hard. Alone and hard. I handled it though. I missed you." My hand sneaks out and pinches her ass cheek.

She squeaks and jumps out of my grip. "God, Lucas, stop!"

I grin at her because I haven't had my fill of her today yet. We walk hand in hand like the perfect looking couple that we are. Living up to our college years and sexy as fuck. Both of us come from well-to-do families, but we also want more out of life than money.

When we reach the car, I toss both of our bags into the back of my Bronco, and we ride together over to my apartment. It's a great place since it's close to campus, and a solid bonus is that my parents pay for it.

As soon as I shut the front door behind us and the bags hit the floor, so do our pants. My hands eagerly rip her clothes off as I'm chasing her around the living room, eventually getting her naked and on her back on the couch. My condom covered dick easily glides in and out of her. She gasps and pulls me into her body with her legs.

"Fuck yes, fuck me, Lucas."

I pound her cunt like an Olympic Gold Medal winner as I'm holding back the release that's been begging to be unleashed. Her little pussy clenches around me, and I explode, unable to stop anymore.

"F-u-c-k," I pant and fold over her, grinding one or two more times before pulling out to get rid of the condom.

I snap out of it when Blade and Axl slide onto the barstools next to me.

"Stryker wants us running a load up to Reno," Blade informs me.

"Hell to the fucking yeah."

I'm more than ready. After patching into the club five months ago, the road has done nothing but help me get my mind off that cunt, Ava. Live the high times and forget the family that pushed me away and the woman who sure as fuck didn't deserve me.

A month later after that day, I found out that she was engaged, and had been since Christmas, to her high school boyfriend who was about to graduate from law school. I was her side piece, someone to fuck away the time with and ride my dick and bike for kicks. It still stings, but fuck it, better to find out now than later.

My parents learned about our split and wanted me to go home back to California, finish my business degree there so that I could work with my dad and take over his company eventually. When they found out that their son had been patched in as a 'gang member', they disowned me. It's not good for business with men in expensive slick suits. Since then, I haven't felt freer from the social obligations and inheritance and what all that meant.

Axl smiles and lifts a bottle of beer, clinking it to mine, "Bitches and brew, brother."

"The B's of life, boobs, bacon, beer, bitches and Battle Born." We chug our beer and head over to the pool tables. Club pussy saunters up to the three of us. They rub their tits or ass over our bodies while we shoot pool and take hits off a pipe that's packed with skunk weed.

My mind drifts off to dirty deeds and the hot young piece of ass asking, no, scratch that, begging for my dick, when she grabs a handful of it. I sink the last ball and toss the pool stick up on the table. She giggles when I remove her panties and sit her on the edge. My pants fall to the floor and I grab a condom from the nearby table, ripping it open.

"Play with your tits," I bark at her, and she does unbashfully.

Her petite hands roll her nipples around in circles, and the latex rolls down my stiff, eager shaft, all the way to the base. She moans when I grip her hips and shove myself into her hot, wet cunt. Trixie loves to take my dick and others'. Two at a time, however we want it, she gives it.

"You better rub that clit if you want to come, Trix." She's my main bang bunny.

My fazing mind starts to catch up with what went through my head just as I start to come. Axl sets up the balls in the tringle and points at my reddening face, "What's so funny?"

A deep roar of laughter comes out of me, "Bang bunny."

Blade and Axl laugh along because they are as high as I am, and we spend the night finding more B words before we take off on a run up north. A van stocked with coke and weed to be delivered, and green cash ready to be brought back to Stryker.

I love my brothers and the club. Fuck my parents and the rest. Living high and living how I want, free, that's where it's at.

Hungover as fuck, the next morning at dawn, after only two hours of sleep, the three of us walk out of the clubhouse only to come face to face with a very pissed off Stryker and an amused Maddox, both standing out front by the van.

"You fuckheads even sober?" Stryker growls at us. Blade, the master of disguises, looks the most put together after the three of us smoked weed, fucked and drank all night. Axl and I wince at his deep voice.

"We are good," Blade easily lies and takes the keys from his old man.

"Axl," Maddox calls, "You gotta slow down, son, when you have runs. Keep your mind sharp for the club." He shakes his head and pulls Axl in for a hug. "Quit being a stud and leave that dumb shit for later, yeah?"

Axl smirks and takes a step back, "No worries, Mad, the boys and I got this, it's an easy run."

Blade tosses me the keys and Stryker gives us the drop off locations, sending the information to our flip phones. We load the van, and, as soon as we are out of sight, Axl curls up in the back and Blade passes out next me.

Motherfuckers.

We spend the next few years just like this, in a blaze of fun as newly patched-in members earning our dues. Memories I know I will take with me to my grave. Like the day I met Axl and Blade as a young kid in sixth grade, looking to score a bag of bud and these two sold it to me. Shortly, Spider met up with our crew, and the four of us have been inseparable ever since. Spider's always a moody fucker too.

Later on, we made some serious cash supplying the kids at the college parties and they knew who to call. My clueless, uptight parents left Vegas for California about the time college started, but there was no way they could take me out of Nevada.

Axl, Blade and Spider did not give a shit about school. I only went so that I could get cash off the parents and didn't have to work.

It worked out as it was meant to, though.

Eventually, I got them to hang around for a few parties, and was making college an epic, never ending party. I bought a bike and Blade taught me how to ride. All my college classes became geared around mechanics and I kept up only a few credit courses in business. That came in handy for the club later, too.

I never did graduate, not that I cared because I knew I had found my way. The B's of life, bands, bank, bud, bitches, beer and bikes.

I found the road that was only meant for me, a road dog.

CHAPTER 2

Katherine

Mexico City, About three years ago...

I gasp for air. I can't seem to find enough to fill my lungs. My nails claw into his back, hopefully hard enough to draw blood.

"Katherine," Matias rasps, his lips grazing the shell of my ear. His breath feathers across my heated neck. "Don't disobey me again."

My head is held firmly in place while he crushes me under him. I'm about to black out and see spots, but I try to fight it.

The sick fuck loves it when I give in and he wins. It's a twisted game we started all those years ago. He's punished me ever since the day we married, not only with his hands and body, but he has also crushed my dreams and suffocated the softer part of me until it died.

He continues pounding into my cunt, selfishly chasing his release.

The devil finally lets go of my throat by releasing his iron grip, and the world stops just for a moment while I gasp for air and my head spins. His deep laughter fills the space and echoes across the room, making him sound like a maniac. I start coughing in between the deep breaths that I take.

Matias pauses for a moment from his punishing pace to lick my nipples and suck them into his mouth. For a second, it's a glimpse of the lover that I thought I had.

As he pulls out of me and trails kisses down my stomach, I mourn the loss of something I never acquired and the game I lost at, love.

Control.

He is the king of manipulation, playing mind games, and beating me at it at a young age, but I've learned so much since then. I let him have this moment, taking my flesh any which way as he wishes.

His tongue aggressively laps at my clit, and he groans. The vibration adds to the intensity and to my pleasure. He proceeds relentlessly until my body completely betrays me and I come for him. He has a firm grip on my hips as he flips me over onto my hands and knees, slapping my ass before gripping my ponytail and pulling me back, arching me painfully to him.

"Don't fucking wear that black dress again. You are my wife, not my whore when we're in public." Spitting his hatred at me, he pulls my hair harder before impaling my body with his dick. Behind me, he pounds out his frustrations with his steal cock.

The tears never come anymore and have been long gone now for years. Love and feelings are something I do not possess anymore, and that's just how he wants me.

Minutes pass while I'm being fucked, and my scalp is on fire from where he's tugging on my hair. Finally, he comes, and releases his hold. I collapse forward onto our bed and force my muscles to relax when he curls up behind me.

"Shower and wear the lotion I bought you, I want you to smell good," he squeezes my side. "*Te amo para siempre, mi amor.* I have to work late."

He expects the words back out of respect for him and the man that he is, Cartel. "*Te amo mucho.*" The words taste sour, but, like a machine, I give them to him.

"*Bueno*, good."

He rises from the bed and zips up his pants, then tucks his shirt back in. Never does he appear disheveled or un-kept. In the mirror above the dresser, he slicks his black hair back and combs through his goatee. Lastly, he straightens his tie and catches me watching him. The devil that holds my thoughts and life captive.

His sinfully dark eyes gleam at my naked body from the reflection he sees there, and he grins. "Fuck, I love your body, be ready for me to fuck it later. I wasn't hard enough on you today. Never satisfied."

Abruptly, without any further thought for me, he turns around and leaves the room to go back downstairs to the Cartel members who are waiting for him. More business to be discussed and finished. I, however, am just a toy, something to be played with.

A week ago, he demanded that I arranged an elaborate dinner here for his associates and his father who is also the Cartel boss. Doing exactly as I was told, I performed as he wished and prepared the evening to dazzle the men and fawn over him. All to show off his wealth and status but also me, his trophy and submissive in bed.

This morning, a package arrived, and, inside, there was a delicate silky black dress with a note from him.

Wear this tonight for me, mi amor.
Matias

For a split second, butterflies of excitement swarmed inside, and I thought he was sincere, until I saw the back. The plummeting cut was dangerously close to showing my backside. My hopes plummeted too, and I knew then that he'd set me up to fail this evening. Matias gets hard testing everyone around him and setting you in his trap.

My weakened body screams at me when I push off the bed and pick up the ruined dress that he ripped off me, then walk into the bathroom. I toss it away into the trash and turn to stare at the large mirror above the sink. Some things can't be tossed away like the dress. The *ruined* feeling sticks like a leach that's sucking away anything that's possibly beautifully bright.

Gasps leave me at the sight of my neck that is red from the marks left over from him strangling me, and my arms are starting to bruise. Even though the pain physically starts to set in, my heart is different. Numb is how I feel in this moment and how I've been feeling for years after giving into his demands. My black eyeliner has run down my cheeks, and I hate the woman looking back at me. She hates the pathetic creature standing here, giving in.

Ignoring the hollowness in my chest, I wash him away with a hot shower and scrub until it burns. On auto pilot, I soothe my skin by rubbing on the lotion Matias requested before pulling a silk nighty over my head.

A shaky hand lifts the glass of water that's sitting on my nightstand, and I walk over to the dresser, glancing at the pictures that I have displayed there. My finger draws a line over the sixteen-year-old girl and the young man standing next to her. Proudly holding her to his side, and she peers up at him as he's looking down into her eyes. So young and so stupid.

Not that I had much choice.

A memory takes over, off to a time when I was a young woman, so in love, or so I thought.

The back of mi papa's hand comes down and slices across my face. If I could cry, I would, but I refuse to show this asshole that kind of ownership over me anymore. The sting spreads like fire across my cheek and heart. He and I glare at each other, waiting for the other to break first. Papa raises a brow and then slowly his arm, up as high as he can across his body, to slap me again.

I can't see past anything but the hate we exchange in our icy stare.

"Cobra." A younger man steps out from behind me and pushes Papa back, getting in between the two of us. I didn't hear or see that he had arrived with the others. The men my father deals with regularly, the Mexican Cartel.

"Fucking touch her face again, pinche pendejo, *and we'll see if* mi padre *won't let me kill you."*

Cobra doesn't move a muscle other than the sneer on his face for me, his prized daughter. Who is to be sold off like a mule. The glare in my eyes would kill him on its own if it could.

The mask comes down and hides the real man wearing it. Cobra. El Presidente de Los Reyes Malditos. *The president of the Cursed Kings, Mexican MC, the man responsible for trafficking millions of dollars in drugs.*

"Con permiso, pinche ninás, sí! Excuse me, foolish daughters, yes? Come, let's have tequila and go over business in my office before the party begins."

He flashes his winning smile over to me and walks like a king, herding his associates with him down the hallway.

"Katherine," the stranger turns to me with fire in his eyes.

I may be turning only fifteen in a month, but I know and have witnessed enough to realize that what I'm seeing on his face is lust. He doesn't touch my face or skin because it is forbidden to touch a virgin. The guards that stand around would tell mi papa, *and I would be punished for allowing it.*

"Behave like the bonita mujer *that you are. We don't want such a beautiful face to be bruised on your* quinceañera, *sí?" His eyes devour me from my eyes, to my lips and then down to my chest and legs, then back up again.*

My head falls to the side, and I analyze the man I have never seen walking through the doors of the casa. *I would remember such a handsome, commanding man.*

"No, señor. *Could I have your name, please?" I go for gracious with the stranger. He would desire it, and I do want to know more. How does he know me, and why does he care if my father slapped me?*

"Matias Castillo," he simply states and waits for my reaction, but I give him none. It is as I suspected, he is the son of the Cartel boss.

He left me standing there with tempting thoughts I couldn't do anything with.

My father came for me that night. He made me kill a whore with a knife. I had to slit her throat for having run away. *Mi padre* spat in my face after to remind me that I would be next if I made a scene like that again. He knew I hated killing women, but he made me.

I didn't run into Matias again after that night. The dangerous stranger was stuck in my mind like a virus. I wanted more of him and his devilish good looks. I knew he probably wasn't good for me, and I forced myself to forget in the next few weeks that passed after our run in.

My throat constricts and my eyes squeeze tightly as I'm taken back into the past.

The church bells ring off into the distance and the sounds of birds scattering and flying away filter into the car. Korina and I laugh as we giggle and whisper our hopes for one of the birds to shit on the people that have gathered for our quinceañera.

Since the death of our mother, she and I have only gotten stronger in our connection, and my father hates that. At least it seems that he does, and I don't understand why. Pushing past the thought, I focus on our special day.

Together, we get out of the car and she helps with fluffing out my white dress. I haven't felt like a princess in so long, and, in this moment I do. I allow myself to live in this dream for today and today only. I know better. The dress makes me look like the happiest girl in the world, where lies live beneath the large bell-shaped dress with its over-the-top puffy sleeves.

Mi papa comes around the car, and, for the crowd, he waves before placing an attentive kiss on my cheek. He then pulls back with an adoring smile, taking my hand and gently placing it on his arm. He does the same for Korina, situating her on his other arm.

The girls that came with us for the ceremony pamper Korina, fluffing out the dress she wears which is identical to my own. They all chose to match and wear sleek lilac dresses. Like a walk down the aisle, the girls follow behind and we smile proudly for everyone to see.

The priest waits for Korina, my father and I to approach the front of the church where the ceremony is to take place. It is witnessed by the large crowd that has turned out to pay respects to our family. The entire time the priest talks and gives his blessing for us to start dating, I can only think about the man who defended me, Matias. Will he come looking for me now, after today?

Soon enough, after the church ceremony, we leave to go back to our family's large home and ranch. El Banda Machos *play in the back yard and the beat pumps up the crowd along with beer, tequila and the drugs that are discretely passed around. But I ignore all of that and hang out with my friends and cousins. We sneak a few shots of tequila, eat until we can't possibly eat anymore and dance for hours until the main event is here.*

Mi papa *wouldn't tell me who the* chambelans, *the young men who will lead my sister and I through the traditional dance to celebrate our age in becoming women and ready to date, would be.*

The music changes to the song we practiced weeks for, and the girls line up behind us, with each of them being paired with a boy. Nerves overcome me at who my father could have chosen for me.

A strong confident hand glides over my forearm and clasps my hand.

"Hola, mi Katherine, you are so very beautiful."
Matias.

My breath hitches, and I turn to face him. He is so close, we are mere inches from a kiss. Before either of us can do anything, the beat picks up and we do as we are instructed, dancing across the floor together. Giving the crowd a great show with our performance.

I don't know how we did it. Our eyes never left the other and I fell in love with him that night. The stars shown as bright as my future, and magic seeped into our hearts.

Only, I fell in love with the lies and deceit that I never saw coming because I allowed myself to believe in fairytales.

On that day when I first saw Matias, my father gave him a contract for my hand in marriage. Cobra, my old man, had sold me off to the Cartel, to form alliances with them.

A year later, after my *quinceañera*, I was engaged to Matias, and he took my virginity that night. I desperately wanted him to. I wanted him so badly to claim me and possess me.

I didn't see him much because he worked a lot. But now, looking back after years have passed, I chuckle. Yeah, he was busy fucking anything he could.

By my eighteenth birthday, I was married to the man of my dreams who ended up being a nightmare that came to life.

Possess me he did, the cold calculated virus that lived in him, now living in me.

I married the man known in the Cartel as *El Psicópata*.

The Psycho.

CHAPTER 3

Katherine

A car backfiring in the busy street of Mexico City forces me to jump from the obnoxious sound behind me as I'm getting out of the our car. My nerves flare, and panic sets in before the guards step in closer to me and my sister, Korina.

The bustle of the packed sidewalk of people goes on unfazed. But to the *Familia* Castillo, enemies are everywhere and everyone. You would think, after nine years of being married to the Cartel, I would not have reacted this way, but things have felt a little off lately.

Not only am I older, and my twenty-eighth birthday is coming up, but my life doesn't feel settled. Korina has grown increasingly cold and distant. My father has been calling me more than the usual. He has news and it must be why Matias has ordered for Korina to stay near us this week. He doesn't trust my father, and he shouldn't.

Cobra always has plans, and that's why, over the years, I've kept up my boxing and running. However, with the change in the surroundings, I've increased my exercises and time at the gun range. This morning, I ran an extra two miles and then kick boxed with my trainer for hours. I didn't stop until my arms and legs couldn't make another swing or kick without falling.

As I'm walking around inside a cute boutique, a thought sticks with me. Why are the guards so jumpy as well? For me, that's a normal reaction, but it's as if they are waiting for something. I watch for any further signs while we continue our browsing in the shop, wandering over to the lingerie section where I can keep an eye on the front door and everyone else that's in the store.

My fingers trail over the lace of a blood red corset, it's beautiful. I can't help myself from soaking in the details, taking in every stich. Desire burns in my heart to wear it, but I won't buy it for Matias. He would just ruin it.

"Korina, are you happy with your life?" I wonder out loud and memories play in my mind like a movie. A daydream of what it all could have been like had I been someone different. What if I hadn't been the daughter of Cobra?

Korina has never married, but I really wonder if she is happy. I find it strange that she has not found a husband, or, rather, that our father hasn't arranged one for her.

"Sí, why wouldn't I be?" she questions. A sigh escapes me; I don't know that she would get where I am coming from. Our father never contracted her into marriage like he did me. Korina would never know how cruel Matias can be.

"I sometimes wonder what it would have been like to have been able to choose my life differently, what it would've been like now," I shrug. "Doesn't matter really—"

My thoughts die out when I catch her staring over to the car that just pulled up, and Esteban steps out to speak with a guard. Korina is intently watching every step he takes.

"You see something you like?" I tease. Esteban is dark and handsome, has a goatee, and is Matias' right hand man.

She shakes her head no and looks back over to me, "Not all of us are free to choose, Katherine." Her voice has a bite to it, more than ever before.

Why would she think that I was free to choose? Or is she implying that she couldn't choose?

She takes her bras and underwear over to the cashier when she sees Esteban walking over to us.

"Matias wants you back at the *casa*, along with Korina." His eyes wonder over my sister's body, then quickly directs them back to me.

"*Sí*, Esteban, can we stop at the market for groceries or is this urgent?"

"We need to hurry, *tu padre esta en la casa*."

If my father is at the house, then he has business there, and my heart sinks at what he would want. It is never good.

Korina walks over to us and Esteban steps protectively close to her side, escorting her to his car and not to the one she and I came in together.

The guard opens my door and I slip into the seat, staring out the window, watching the people on the crowded street. Busy with their lives. Children keeping up with their mothers. I wonder if they're happy.

My thoughts jump back to when my mother was still alive, and I was a little girl.

"Tell me, Katherine, what does mi hija *want to be when she grows up?" My mother runs her hand through my hair while she lies next to me on my bed. I stare into her deep brown eyes that have light wrinkles around them.*

"One day I want to be a momma just like you and have a husband to love me. Maybe I could be a nurse too and take care of people." Her hand stills in my hair and she closes her eyes briefly before opening them to look at me. Her breathing changed and I feel bad. Did I disappoint her?

"What's wrong, momma?" My hand grabs her arm and she tries to smile, but I know her, she is sad.

"Don't forget your dreams, mi hija, *promise me?"*

"Sí, momma, please don't be sad. I'm sorry," I beg her. I want her to smile more.

"Don't be, mi bebe. Ven aca, *come here." She pulls me back to her and wraps a protective arm around my body. "Go to sleep, my baby, dream of your world. I want you to have that so much."*

Her whispering voice cracks at the end and I feel even worse that I upset her. Holding her tight, I try to make up for my mistake.

The voices outside carry on through the night. Men and women laughing from the beer and tequila they're drinking. I don't care because she makes me feel safe, and I drift off to sleep in her arms.

The car comes to a stop and I'm jolted out of my dream. I gather my bags and step out to a not so happy looking Matias. I don't even pay attention anymore, as he is never happy.

He grabs the bags from my hands, and I lean in to kiss his devastatingly handsome face that I used to die to see.

"*Gracias, mi amor,*" I politely thank him and wait for what he wants from me.

He wraps his arm around my body and the contact hurts with the void that is now there. He whispers into my ear, "Make your *padre* happy tonight, don't fuck this up with your attitude," he warns me and pecks my cheek, then a little louder he plays his part as *mi padre* steps out the front door. "Love you too, *mi amor.*" I turn to him with my eyes shut and push forward to kiss his lips.

"Katherine." My father tilts his head to me, and I nod. The words feel stuck in my throat before Matias' hand grips my arm painfully.

"Papa, I'm so happy you are here. What can I make you for dinner?" The vomit I feel lodged in my throat from the bullshit coming from my mouth is nauseating, a sickening feeling in my stomach. Cobra smiles that I have finally found my manners and have given into what is expected of me.

"Whatever you have is fine," he concedes with a dismissive look.

"Okay, I'll have something ready soon." Matias loosens his biting grip, and I leave them outside before I do something that will make things worse for me.

In my room, I drop the bags like bricks, my day of shopping losing its luster of my usual escape.

After a moment of gathering and bracing myself for the night ahead, I make a mental list of my tasks and head into the kitchen to begin preparing dinner. My feet start to ache in these heels, but I know better than to take them off.

I hear men talking in the hallway and tiptoe over to listen. "Where is she now? Why did you take so long?" Matias growls.

"I drove around to make sure there was no tail on Katherine. I distracted them, and they followed me," Esteban replies patiently to his boss.

"Do not fucking take Korina alone again. She stays here tonight, until all threats are cleared." The harshness in his voice and odd command makes my head snap back like a slap to the face.

Quickly, I tiptoe back over to the sink and turn on the faucet to wash my hands. The door swings open into the kitchen and I hum along to a song, pretending that I didn't hear the conversation from just seconds ago.

Matias storms in and starts pacing the floor in front of the island. I walk over to the fridge and pull out a beer for him, then step closer to hand it to him.

He snatches the bottle from me with one hand and grabs my arm with the other, aggressively pulling me into him. My body collides against his chest, making me trip over my heels from the force of his anger.

"You are mine, never forget that," he sneers down at me.

The love that was once in his eyes from when we were young lovers is now distorted into the man he is today. He crashes a brutal kiss on my mouth, then rips away, pushing me back. He storms away from me and out of the kitchen with uncontrollable brutality.

Propelled backward, my back stops my fall as I'm slamming against the kitchen island. Pain shoots through my side and I lose my breath from the wind being knocked out of me. I double over, terrified, trying to breathe through it. Finally, I take a paralyzing gasp of air in, and my eyes water from the intensity. I close them and take deep, calming breaths in.

Moments later, Korina is in the kitchen with me. She doesn't seem to notice my distress, but I clearly see the pain etched on her face. My heart throbs and realization hits when she says, "Matias wants me to help you."

"How long?" my choked-up voice rasps.

Not my sister. God, not her.

"It doesn't matter, Katherine, I didn't choose this," she bites back at me, waving her arm around.

My hands fist at my sides. Hate overwhelms me that he has taken every bit of anything good that I ever had, and that I never tried stopping him.

Like a practiced routine, we bury our problems, and my sister and I work together in a deafening silence.

Nothing will ever be the same again.

All the times our father tricked me into doing horrible things so she wouldn't have to, and, in the end, she betrayed me.

I allow the devastation to eat me whole and consume me with the heartbreaking truth. Once again, I must mourn the loss of someone I love. This is not the sister I know. Hell, I'm not even me for that matter.

Who the hell have we become?

I straighten my spine because I'm going to need it to live through the next few hours without giving away what I know. Fuck, what am I saying? I'm going to need it to survive this to be able to escape this hell alive.

She works besides me like a robot, warming tortillas while I finish plating our dinner. We walk out together, carrying the plates for the men at the table and placing beers in front of them. After they are served, she and I are forced to sit across from each other.

I hate her. Hate that she has done this to me.

My anger is so fierce that I would put a bullet in every single person's head that's sitting at this table. Including my own.

This shit is so fucked up and poisonous. Every single person sitting here represents poison to love and dreams and everything good.

I stare daggers at the bitch that I felt was the only person I could trust.

Mi padre looks between us both, and a light comes on. This just got worse. He will use it to drive me to do what he wants. I just know that he will find a way to use this information to his advantage.

I can't help but seething and glaring at her with disgust. I can feel Matias' eyes boring holes into my skull with his anger. Fuck him, too.

A fire burns hotter within me, and I turn and scowl at him with all the pain that's pent up over the years. Let him see the creature he's turned me into.

His jaw ticks at me, and I squint back at him, a challenge to kill me. *Do it, I have nothing, not a damn thing, to lose anymore.* He has sucked everything good out of me, like a leach.

A smirk comes over my face. "You'll have to excuse me," I comment, wiping my mouth with my napkin, "I feel very nauseous and must go lie down."

I stand and toss my napkin on the table. "*Padre, hermana, esposo,*" I look each one in the eye, "*Te amo tanto, mi familia, buenas noches.*" I tell them how much I love them all, hoping to spread the disdain like cancer.

With that, I leave in silence, knowing that I've created a war, and I could care less.

On the back patio outside of my room, while they finish their dinners, I smoke a cigar as I'm watching the night sky. My back rests against a large pillar and a foot is propped up, keeping me from crumbling.

A long pull and then exhale of the cigar whispers across the sky, and the smoke, like a hypnotic dance, plays before my eyes. The quiet, along with the smoking, calms my nerves while I contemplate my next move.

I think about all the times I was blind to the bullshit happening right under my nose. What I now see as bullshit, it was easier to ignore then, to confront it.

The sliding door opens, and I don't turn my head to know who it is. I wish he would leave and go fuck the whores that I know he fucks and leave me alone.

Matias comes to stand in front of me and rests his hands on each side of my head. He leans in, a breath away from me. My body shivers from his touch when a finger skims over my cheek, not with want, but with the disgust that comes with touching him now.

I can't even finish this in peace, so I blow the smoke into his face. I rest the cigar on the ashtray that's sitting on a table next to me.

"She has never been you. Just another whore to play with." His eyes look into mine. "You understand because you are my wife. You don't need to worry about that. I'll give you the children you've always wanted, Katherine." He pulls my shirt down and places soft kisses over my shoulder and up my neck.

I'm frozen from his words. He would never give me kids before because he wanted to ensure his position and our safety first, he'd always say. It was all bullshit, controlling me like he always had.

He lifts my hand and kisses my ring, then squeezes my fingers. "I remember the first day I saw you, so beautiful, I had to have you. I bargained to take you for my own, away from many others who wanted you."

He stops talking to kiss my ear, then continues in a quiet tone. "The first night I took you as my own... Your tight little pussy was drenched and ready for my dick. You always loved me, Katherine, admit it." He taunts me to deny it, deny the truth.

Searing anger forces my hand back and I surprise him with a slap across the face. "You took a little girl and fed her full of lies and bullshit like you do to gain control of your men." I hold a pointed finger to his face, "I've been nothing but a fucking game and pussy for you to fuck, another whore to you, *mi esposo, el psicópata*, the psycho. Deny the truth, Matias." I drop my hand and wait for the retribution.

My chest heaves with the anger running through my veins. He steps forward and grips my face with his fingers digging into my cheeks. "*Sí, mi hermosa puta.* You were always my beautiful pussy."

He laughs into my face and, for the first time, he allows me to see the real man and the poison that he is.

"You loved all of it." He pulls me toward him and rubs his stiff dick into my stomach. "I'm still going to knock you up and have my kids, and you won't fucking stop me. You'll shut your fucking mouth and be a good little *perra* and do what you're told."

My hands come up to his shoulders attempting to shove him away from me. He laughs again and grabs my hair at the back of my head.

On instinct, I swing a fist and hit him in the face. Blood slowly starts trickling down from his nose. He stops and wipes what he can away. He grins, "Katherine, the last man who hit me is dead." He looks over my face and promises of death appear in his eyes.

"But you won't," I finish for him, "Because there are worse things than death."

The devil snickers into the night air and leans in with his full weight, trapping me, but I refuse to flinch. I won't allow him to scare me.

"*Sí, mi esposa*, I still love you and always will. You were always mine and we were made to rule this world together. You'll see."

His hands come up to my blouse and grips the silky black material, ripping it apart and exposing me to the hot night air. My chest heaves uncontrollably, some sick and twisted part of me allowing it to happen.

Excitement races through him at the exposure of it all, not just my skin but the truth. He presses me harder against the pillar and drags my skirt up my thighs, then shreds my underwear away from me. He forces his pants down just far enough to release his dick.

Strong hands lift me up by the back of my thighs, and then he's shoving himself into me. The excitement captures me as well as the truth, because I know we will die if we stay together. We will kill each other.

I say goodbye to the man I loved and fuck him one last time with what's left of the girl with a heart. I give him everything and remember the man I loved as a young woman. I grip his face and kiss him with my dying devotion. He pumps into me and rubs my clit with one hand until I fall apart in his arms. I climax and shatter apart on what I used to believe were my hope and dreams.

Matias is my poison.

CHAPTER 4

Matias

With one foot resting over my knee, relaxing in my chair in the corner of our bedroom, I watch my wife as she's sleeping peacefully while my eyes roam over her curves. I smoke from the same cigar that she didn't finish earlier. The taste of her lipstick seeps into my mouth, the taste of *her*.

I couldn't let her go all those years after the first time I saw her as a young woman. I had watched her and owned her for years before I purposely walked in on her and her father. Cobra knew in that moment what I was there for. To bargain for his daughter and he was more than happy to sell her to me. She just never knew.

My father wants me to kill her now, and sever business with her father. Make it look like he had one of his men murder her so we can wipe out his MC without questions. He's tired of the *pendejo* and wants to work directly with the Battle Born MC in the States to push the drugs and the export of bitches.

Katherine was always a pawn in our game with her father that I had convinced my own father to pursue. Korina is just a pussy for me to fuck with, unless she becomes valuable at some point. She's not as smart as her sister though and is why I picked Katherine to be my wife.

For the first time in my life, I feel like my wife knows who I am. How I'd always known that she was meant to be mine. Finally, I fucked her like the demon residing inside of me was freed and how I've been dreaming about for years. There is no way I will allow my father to take that away from me now. Katherine is mine to keep and corrupt her heart to match my own.

My dick is rock hard at the thought of the misery pouring from her, into me, and the moment we shared when she gave it back to me fearlessly. The taste of my blood made it that much sweeter, a promise has been made.

She's ready to carry our child and stand behind me now that she knows the truth. She's addicted to me as much as I am to her. We match in every way. She's fucking perfect for me.

Standing up from the chair, I call my brother, Angel, as I step outside on the patio. He answers quickly and I question him, "Are we ready to move forward and take our father out?"

He chuckles, "I'm setting it up. I've been pushing Cobra to gain more traction with Battle Born. Of course, they don't want to work with him and the bad blood that has been spilled between them. Soon, a war will break out and then we will be ready."

I hang up the line without a goodbye and laugh out loud at how perfectly this has lined up. If I got to impregnate Katherine too, all the sweeter and better for my plans. Soon, she'll find out that her last birth control shot had been just a vitamin shot. She could already be carrying my child and there is no way my father will kill her when he finds out he has a grandson on the way. It will make him a little easier to manipulate and distract. Then, I will take my spot where I belong, at the head of the Cartel, with Katherine by my side.

My cock twitches at the sadistic idea of fucking her sister in our house and whether Katherine will figure it out or not. I live for the games I play with her.

I put out the cigar in the ashtray and walk through the house to enter Korina's room. She too is fast asleep.

A short time after I fucked Katherine for the first time, I also took Korina's virginity, and have had her as my mistress for years. Everyone's known about it except for Katherine, until yesterday when she finally figured it out. I will have to kill Korina if she becomes unpredictable.

Now, my gaze roams over her peaceful body, picturing her dead, limp and cold. The fantasy excites me, fueling me to fuck her within an inch of her life. It would feel same as killing my wife, and, someday, I *will* kill Korina in order to keep Katherine safe.

Korina has always disappointed me in that she's been so easy to control, and she played into my hands so easily. But she's also kept an eye on Katherine for me, and would tell me anything I wanted. That's how I knew exactly how to always play my wife.

I tear the blankets away to reveal Korina's naked body, as always. Since she was young, I prepared her sleep this way so I could fuck her and get out.

She startles from her sleep and gasps when I pull her from the bed, her feet hitting the floor, leaving her chest down on top of the mattress.

"Matias, I'm sorry, I don't know how she figured it out," she pleads.

Gradually, I take off my belt and push my pants down, stroking my dick while looking at her cunt.

"Because she's not fucking stupid and you're a weak bitch. You're useless to me now, Korina," I tease her with the truth, and she cries out, her body shaking. The sound makes me harder while I stroke myself.

"I may forgive you, eventually, when I find a new way to get the information I want." I take my belt and loop it around her head and into her mouth to gag her. She doesn't dare to move, she knows what happens when she does, and places her hands behind her back, waiting.

I cover my dick with a condom and, leaning over her, I lunge forward and impale her flesh with my dick. Never do I want her filth on my skin, only my Katherine. I pull back on the belt and fuck Korina hard into the mattress, for my own pleasure. And, fuck, is it good.

"Keep your mouth shut, Korina. You tell her nothing or I'll choke you to death and bury you."

All you can hear is my skin slapping against hers with my brutal thrusts. Saliva drips from her mouth and tears run in rivers and fall down her face, wetting the silk sheets.

I close my eyes and picture Katherine this way. I hope she knows how much I want her like this.

I do it to protect her.

Katherine

There was no way I could sleep with the changes from tonight. My mind constantly runs through scenarios and outcomes. My eyes are shut as I pretend to sleep even though I have been awake for a while now.

I feel it deep into my bones that I am going to die young, like my momma, if I stay. I promised her to live out my dreams, and I'm not. It's time that I fought back and lived. The timing is right. I've waited and watched, and I see it clearly written. It will be the fight of my life.

Matias moves to the patio, and I hear him talking on the phone, saying he's going to take his father out. My mind scrambles, wondering why he would do that. Obviously for the power, but where does that leave my own father? I don't believe in coincidences. Matias brought Cobra here for a reason, and it wasn't a family reunion.

He leaves our bedroom, and, out of curiosity, I silently follow him. I have to control my breathing when I watch him as he enters Korina's room. With my heartbeat drumming in my ears, I tiptoe closer, anxious to hear what's happening in there.

Years of my father forcing me to watch him and his men rape and torture women have paid off. I keep my focus to catalogue what I am seeing and not emotionally check out. I would love nothing more than to put a bullet into each of these useless people.

The words Matias says to Korina tell me so much. I've been so blind to it all, blinded by lust and love. He's used my sister against me for years. My best friend.

I hear him fucking her, and a part of me feels horrible for her while the other part of me hates her. I embrace the hate and the will to outlive this asshole.

Ideas spread into my mind like a disease and, suddenly, revenge looks really good.

Game on, motherfucker.

Matias

I wake up alone and Katherine is nowhere to be found in our bedroom. After I shower and dress in the pantsuit that my beautiful wife laid out for me, I go in search of her and find her sitting at the table for breakfast.

"*Buenos días, mi amor*, good morning, my love, are you working from home today?" she questions as she stands up to get me coffee and then setting the cup down at my place at the table.

I tilt my head to the side and observe her for a moment. Katherine's face remains impassive, and she is dressed head to toe in her favorite color, black. She shows no signs of distress from yesterday.

"No, Katherine, I will be going out," I answer, keeping my voice monotone. Taking a seat, I wait for her to sit as well. This game is exciting, it's new for her. Something changed in her yesterday and I'm genuinely happy with this progress.

"Okay," she simply states with a nod. She takes a few tentative sips of her steaming hot coffee and graciously mentions, "Please eat, Matias. Korina will be a few more minutes before she joins us." Still, she doesn't flinch at her words, and I am impressed. My wife smiles and takes a few bites from her oatmeal.

I hear movement by the door and turn just in time to see Korina sheepishly entering the dining room, enhancing our game at the table, and taking a seat. I know she'll blow this because she's weak.

"Did you have a good night, honey?" Katherine reaches forward and squeezes her sister's hand. As her blouse falls open, her breasts push up with the movement. I never allow Katherine to show her body like this unless I give her permission, and her tits are directed at the guards, giving them a great view of what's fucking mine.

"Um, ye-e-s," Korina stammers and looks away from us both, pulling away from her sister and hurriedly picking up her coffee cup with a shaking hand.

Katherine tsk's her tongue. "You should have mentioned it last night to Matias if you were uncomfortable, please forgive me that I went to bed early."

Korina chokes on her coffee like I knew the bitch would. Goddamn it.

Katherine pulls up the newspaper from the table. "I'm not feeling well. A little nauseated. I'm going to head outside and read the paper. I think the fresh air will help." She stands and bends over to kiss my cheek. "Have a good day, *amor*, please enjoy Korina's company." Her luscious tits threaten to fall out and, again, give my guards an eyeful. Her curvy body struts away and outside, dismissing us both.

Suddenly, I wish I didn't have to work and that I could fuck my wife all day today, and make Korina watch while she's tied up. But this game is an aphrodisiac to my fucked up soul, and I desperately want to see where it goes next. Maybe someday.

On my way out I snarl in Korina's ear, "Keep your fucking mouth shut and keep an eye on her, stay close by."

With my day set, I march out the front door and slide my sunglasses on, ready to make more money.

CHAPTER 5

Tank
Las Vegas

What's the worst thing you can give to a young man? Money. A whole lot of fuckin' money. I've been patched in for a few years now and shit just gets better and better.

We're standing around in the garage, looking at the brand-spanking-new Harley I just purchased off the show room floor. Not a mile on this girl, and, boy, is she freakin' sweet.

Blade, Spider and Axl helped me roll her off the trailer and we are painting the club logo on the side of the gas tank now. Well, Blade is. I am too busy supervising his work, as usual. As a kid, I drew a lot, and now I've been working with this shop on the strip, apprenticing for tattoos.

"Bro, when are you going to give tatts a try? Look at you, motherfucker, you are like the Vincent Van Gogh of our ages. All twisted and moody, artistic, asshole-y and shit." I laugh at the glare I get from him while he starts to dry the paint with a hairdryer. "Just don't cut an ear off. Maybe someone else's that's not mine." I just want to clarify because Blade probably would cut my ear off, the sadistic fuck.

"Axl!" I yell and punch his shoulder, causing him to spill his beer on his Guns N' Roses shirt. "Wake the fuck up, dude. What are you daydreaming about?"

He lets out the most exaggerated sigh. "The girl of my dreams. I can't stop thinking about her." He takes another chug of his beer.

"Brother, it's been years. Do you hear me? *Years* since we've seen her at that concert. It's not likely that you will find her again. She probably doesn't even live around here." My hands fly wide to help point out how ridiculous he is. "Who gets this caught up after one night?"

He shrugs a shoulder and looks over to Blade. Both of us watch while he sprays a clear coat over the Battle Born and wolf logo he painted. "Tank, it will happen, and that will come, mark my words. Your big ass will fall hard."

"Not fuckin' likely."

After the clear coat has been dried, we pull the bike out of the garage, and I finally turn on my new baby. "Damn, you hear that?" The engine roars underneath, pushing out a calming purr.

"What time is it, boys?" I yell out to the members that have gathered around us.

"Road Dog time," the boys yell out and jump on their own bikes. The large yard vibrates with the roar from the bikes and our howling. Stryker and Maddox join the crew to baptize my girl on the road, a tradition that started many years ago, and Stryker is adamant that it's good luck for the crew.

Stryker's Ol' Lady, Moxie, wraps her fine body around our Prez, and Harley... Let me just pause this thought here. Harley is a fucking knockout. She has starred in many of my spank bank fantasies. She's better than Mrs. Jones on your street, it's a level above that. Long, dark hair and golden skin. Mad Max, the VP, took one look at her, was hooked, and she was patched into holy biker matrimony within a month.

But back to where we were at. Harley walks down the steps in a pair of leather shorts, thigh high boots, a black Battle Born tank and her MC cut. Bitch swings one leg over and settles into her man. Lucky old ass prick.

The engines rev and the Prez leads the way to Sin City to baptize the newest bike into the club on the Las Vegas Strip. It's always a crowd pleasure when Battle Born takes the road. Cameras come out and pictures of us are taken. It makes my dick a little hard because yeah, we are the big dogs rollin' in.

We end up on Fremont Street and park our bikes up in a garage, then head down to a strip club for drinks and dames for the night.

You know that worse thing you could ever give to a young man, money? I have stacks of it to celebrate. Selling shit has never been better and collections from the other clubs are up. I sit at the front table next to the stage, and place my brick stacks of dollar bills down, ready to pay these girls' college tuitions.

I'm so happy, I can't even wipe the grin off to cover my white teeth. Also, the joint I just smoked could be adding to that. Axl gave me, Blade and Spider a red headband to tie around our heads. We support his strange obsession with them.

The crew and I take up the whole VIP section when the bell rings, alerting the girls that they have special guests to entertain. The bass pumps louder and the stripper parade begins. I rub my hands together excitedly, anticipating my treats for the night.

Blade whistles for one of the girls' attention, so I pass the bouncer a hundred. The buxom brunette gives him a salacious lap dance that's meant to make him come in his pants. He whispers into her ear and she leads him to a private room. Happy endings exist in Vegas only when you have cash, and, well, when you're us.

I'm lost in laughter when I hear Axl asking one of the girls who's dancing on his lap if she has ever been to a Guns N' Roses concert. Maddox and Harley must've heard it over the music too because I can hear them both chuckling about it.

Blade joins us after his seven minutes in heaven and sits down with a fresh cold beer. I'm about to harass him over his quick return when the wind is knocked out of my lungs.

Ava.

She's grinding her perky little body around the pole, all the way down to the floor. She's crawling on all fours while collecting dollar bills before she reaches me and my shit eating grin.

"Well, well, well, look who just came crawling back to me."

Ava's face pales once her eyes look up to see me with my arms crossed over my chest.

"Hey," she lamely greets me while her hands hesitantly crawl up my chest, rubbing them back and forth. "What have you been doing?"

"Blondes, redhead and brunettes."

Blade and Axl roar in laughter behind me and Spider kicks the back of my leg. Warning me to stay away from her, I'm sure.

"Mmm," she hums, trailing her hands over my muscled arms. "Got one for me? For old times' sake?"

I think about her offer to fuck her for free and decide that I am all for that shit. I help her off the stage and flip off the stunned faces watching me walk away her. She leads us into one of the VIP rooms where I let her dance around the pole while she strips out of her barely there white lingerie.

"Where have you been, Ava?" I question and take a seat in a chair.

"I came back to Vegas a few months ago. Things didn't work out in California," she responds as she's twirling around, facing me. "I'm happy I ran into you though." Opening her legs while talking, she slides her back down the pole and pulls her g-string to the side to run her small fingers through her pussy.

"Why is that?"

She saunters over, naked, with a waxed pussy and her red heels on. "Because I always regretted leaving things between us the way they we did."

I want to laugh at how hysterical that is. When she left me, I was getting ready to be patched in and she was engaged to another man. I was ready to brand her as my Ol' Lady that night and she left me hanging, alone. See, funny the way she left things.

"Make up for it then."

She gets down on her knees and pulls my jeans down my legs, finding a few condoms in my back pocket. She tears one off and holds onto it while she takes my dick down to the back of her throat.

My knees open a little wider and my hand finds the back of her head, pumping her up and down on my cock. Her hot mouth sends tingles up my spine.

"Fuck me, Ava."

She opens the wrapper and places the condom on the tip of my dick before her mouth slides it over it. I hiss out from pleasure as I feel her breath heating the rubber and her teeth grazing my cock. Once she has the condom rolled down, she stands and straddles me on the chair, slowly lowering, seating herself on my dick. "Rub your pussy until you come and then you can make me come."

She sticks two fingers into my mouth, and I roll my tongue around them before she gently caresses her clit. She rocks back and forth and begs me to take her back, that she misses me. I let her show go on because, let's face it, her words mean shit. My dick is hard and the woman is fucking hot. I may as well use her hot cunt for the night.

Ava purrs out her release and begins to move up and down, gaining excitement back in her for another climax. Before she gets another one, I grip her hips and pound out my release. Satisfied, I slap her ass.

"Thanks, doll, it was nice running into you."

Her eyes bug out. "What did you just say?"

Picking up her scrawny ass off me, I gently set her on her feet. While I pull the condom off and zip up my pants, I repeat her last words, "I thought we were just having fun," then point between us, "You didn't think this was real, did you? You did, that's so sweet."

Ava stands there with wounded pride and a deflated ego. Can't say I care because she doesn't deserve anything more from me. Because of her, I will never trust that a woman cares for anyone but herself, and I'm never letting any woman on the back of my bike ever again.

"Take care," I call out and head back out to the boys to get the fuck out of here before she creates drama.

Karma is my best friend, and my night has been blessed. Not that I have anything against a girl who wants to strip, but Ava thought she had her life planned out with some rich dick that she had. When that didn't work out, she wanted to crawl back to me. That shit will never happen.

I feel a whole lot like a king and not her or anyone else can stop the awesomeness that's wrapped up in this hot package.

CHAPTER 6

Katherine

I look around the place that I used to call home and see nothing truly memorable that I'd cherish. I'm a stranger in this place, lost to its freshly revealed chaos. I didn't recognize how deep I was in until now, and it may be too late.

It is a sad realization to how much I've lost over the years, or, have I really lost? Maybe now I am seeing clearly for the first time in my life, a light that finally shines bright.

It's time to move on.

My heart takes me on a walk, and I look over the property, remembering the time Matias fucked me in the grass all those years ago. The young girl in me loved it at the time and welcomed him into my body. Years that passed have tarnished the reality of that day. That man manipulated the young girl that I once was, and she has grown numb to him. I never saw him coming with his charms and manipulation.

Sitting down next to the bushes we planted shortly after we built this house, I lie on my back to look up at the sky. The absurdity of all this shit strikes me profoundly. I was groomed the way Matias wanted me to be. I have allowed my father to manipulate me as well. All the shooting, killing and fighting he had me train for was for this moment. After my mother died, he used me for this moment only. To sacrifice me for money.

I chuckle while watching the clouds drift by. My father made sure I was taught to manipulate and outsmart most men. I helped to patch up his club members and assist the doctors. He taught me to shoot guns and throw knives. There wasn't anything my old man didn't teach me. I was an arsenal for him for when the time came that he'd need to use me.

Korina and I moved to the United States with our mother for a few years and went to school in California. We learned English very well, we both spoke it like natives. My father wanted to ensure that all necessary steps were taken so that we would blend in any environment without raising any suspicion, even if he had to send us on a so-called mission to America.

Korina never took his teachings seriously, and, over time, he started ignoring her. Not me though, I soaked up the attention. A part of me loved the dark and cynical world he shared with me.

Speaking of dear old dad, I hear footsteps behind me and then I sense his presence as he's taking a seat next to me. His heavy cologne wafts over me and I don't have to turn my head to just know that it's him.

"Katherine, are you ready now?"

I close my eyes tight. He's come to me like he told me he would, when the time was right.

A memory instantly hits me like a thunder strike, back to the day before my wedding...

Korina calls for me from across the yard. "Katherine! Papa wants you again in his office," she shouts, and I run over to her.

I snort at her attitude, "You think I like being called in there?"

She at least has the decency to look a little sad. I get her disappointment because all she ever really craves is love from our father. I always protect her though, and never tell her what he wants or what he has me do. I could tell her, but it wouldn't be good for either one of us. Our father would beat us both and she would have to endure the same things I have.

I squeeze her shoulder and walk past her to enter his office, then shut the door behind me. I take a seat in a chair in front of his desk and patiently wait.

"Papa, you called for me...?" I finally inquire.

When he's ready, he looks up from the papers he's holding and directs a pointed glare at me. "Tomorrow you will marry into the Cartel." He sits back and looks me in the eyes, not letting my gaze leave him. "You will need to remember everything I taught you over the years. One day, you will do what you are told, without question."

I swallow through the fear of what he is implying.

"I-I love Matias, Papa, please don't make me do something to him!" I plead, pushing my body forward. I would get on my knees and beg at this point.

My father's gut-wrenching laughter fills the air around us. "You think he loves you, pinche puta? *Do you know how many whores he fucks? Katherine," he leans over his desk at me, "Don't be a fucking* perra estupida, *stupid bitch. I taught you so much better." He raises his hand, and I flinch. "Fuck up and Korina will be the whore that pays.* Tu entiendes, *you understand?"*

"Sí, Papa, entiendo," *is all I can answer right this minute, and I pray that the day never comes.*

Opening my eyes to the present, I turn my head to look at my father, but really only seeing a man that I hate. "Sí, Papa, *que necesitas*, what do you need?"

My father's satisfied gleam and smirk approve of my choice of words. What do I have to lose at this point? I need to use my father for what I want, which is a way out.

"Be the wife he wants, not too easy. Get close to him and start feeding me information."

"What is it that you want? What information?"

Cobra's glare cuts off my questions. "Fucking anything, Katherine. I don't explain myself to women, do as you're told."

He gets up from the grass and leaves the property without going back through the house. I glance up and notice that Korina is standing by the window, watching us.

I sit up and huff out a breath, thinking over what my father would want from Matias. More drugs? More money? He can't be stupid enough to expect more than what he's already getting, even possibly rip off a transport.

The more I know on both sides of this, the better. How much can I get involved and survive? It doesn't matter because this is no life, but I will take out as many of these *cabrones* with me as possible.

I get up from my spot and walk into the house, deciding to stop and grab some water from the kitchen. As soon as I walk in, I see Korina glaring at me from the other side of the room. "What was *he* here for?"

"He stayed the night here, Korina," I wave a hand toward her.

"You and I both know he doesn't just *visit* with you." She points a perfectly polished red nail at me.

I snort at her, "Nope, he doesn't." I tilt my head at her. "Why does that make you angry though?"

Korina's eyes dart around. "Doesn't matter, I'm taking off." She storms off, leaving me alone in the kitchen. She now sees me as the enemy. Our father has never had time for her. Does she think that she'll protect Matias by warning him? Korina doesn't understand these games and that Cobra will kill her.

It's become clear that she already is or *will* be a spy for Matias. No, she *is* his spy. All these years, he played on my feelings so easily. He could read me so well, and that's because she'd tell him everything about me. She's been betraying me.

Pain worse than anything I've ever felt slices my heart. I always loved her, she's been my only friend for years. Matias slowly isolated me. He methodically took a piece of me at a time and chipped away all the support I was getting from any good people or things in my life.

Son of a bitch. Pain is instantly replaced with a burning rage and need to get even. This asshole doesn't really know who he is fucking with. It's time to sharpen my skills and get my edge back, bringing *me* back.

As all these thoughts slam into my brain, one thing is clear. I pull out my phone and type a text out to my father.

Me: Thanks for coming, can you meet me for lunch tomorrow? I would like to apologize in person.

I hope he gets what I'm saying without me actually saying it.

Cobra: Be at El Rey, noon

Behind the scenes, I have lots of things to do. I need to get busy setting my own traps. With that in mind, I first go through Matias' office to see if I can find anything useful. His computer is password protected, and logging into it would set off an alarm to his security team.

Next, I rummage through the few papers on his desk. There's nothing that will help me right now other than the name of a shipping company. I place the papers back on the desk and walk over to his printer to check the memory.

I print the documents he hasn't erased and spend an hour getting to know my husband a little better. I even pour myself a shot or two of tequila as I read through the small stack of papers. These, however, only show a schedule of shipments of something that's to be crossed over the border. I flip a page over and see that the next one is a document listing a motorcycle club in the U.S. as a contact. Somebody by the name of Stryker is listed as the president of the Battle Born MC in Las Vegas, Nevada.

Several pictures are attached to it, all showing different people. One of them shows a woman and a man who must be the president and his wife, and it catches my eye, then I look through other pictures of several club members.

So, Battle Born is what my old man was here for last night. Tonight they have a shipment to go load up. I'm sure my father is taking it to them.

This is as good as I'm going to get for today. I move over to the bookcase and find a book with light dust on top. I fold the documents I printed in half before sliding them in between the pages of the book which I then carefully place back on the shelf.

I look around the room for any sign of a false wall or floor but come up empty. He may not hide anything in here.

I don't have time to keep looking, so I decide to move on. I walk into the main part of the house, straight into the officers', or security, area. Quietly, I listen for footsteps but don't hear anything. Someone is down here, there has to be. Room one comes up empty and I slip inside, closing the door behind me without latching it shut.

Rummaging through, I find a switch blade and a credit card. I grin as I stuff both into my boot and pull my pants over to cover it. Knowing not to press my luck further, I tiptoe around the door and back down the hallway when two hands come out of nowhere and wrap around my throat.

"Katherine." His scent overwhelms my senses. My heart pounds into my ears and I feel like I could die in the next few moments.

"What are you doing down here?" He squeezes the hand that's still wrapped around my throat, in warning. "If I catch you fucking my men, I will put a bullet in your traitorous head." His other hand comes around my waist and pulls me into his body.

A second is all I need, I reassure myself, then close my eyes, exhaling the nerves out. I can do this.

My head falls back as I press my ass back into him, grinding into his quickly hardening cock. "I would never betray *tu amor* and respect for me, *mi esposo*. I promised you everything for the same from you in return." My voice sounds scratchy from his hold around my throat.

Matias' grip tightens on my hip, and he grinds back into me. "You want to flash these tits at my men, *mi amor*?" His hand lets go of my throat, then rips the blouse away from my body. Buttons fly and scatter everywhere before he pushes me against the wall. His hand grips the hair at the back of my neck, forcing the side of my head to rest against the wall. My cheek is burning from the pressure.

"You know it's just you and me. It's always been only about you and me, no matter what."

His meaning is clear. He loves me even though he fucks whoever he feels like. It used to be enough, but it's not anymore. I feel betrayed that he would fuck my sister and use her against me for his own sick pleasure.

He kisses my jaw reverently, in contradiction with his painful hold. He ever so lightly whispers, "Maybe I should fuck you in this hallway and let the men watch?"

Rage overwhelms my reaction and my elbow flies back, hitting his side. Not enough to hurt him but it startles him enough that I can shove him away from me.

"I will never be your *puta*," I spit at him. "I am not afraid either to put a bullet in *your* traitorous dick."

Before the last word can leave my mouth, Matias' backhand strikes my cheek and the sting from the slap reminds me of who he is. Once again, he pushes me against the wall and pulls my pants down to my knees.

The sound of his own pants being opened echoes in the empty hallway before he harshly pushes himself into me and rams into my body.

"You have always been my *puta*, whore."

He slams into me and fucks me with no reprieve. Soon, he empties himself while my legs burn from the exertion of him fucking me with all his power. My arms shake against the wall, and I'm about to collapse when he pulls me back to him, cradling me to his body.

"I love you, Katherine, I came home just to fuck you. I missed you so much. I would never allow anyone to see your naked body. Keep it covered."

Swallowing my pride, I nod and let him have this one. I can't win them all, I tell myself. "*Sí*, Matias."

"*Bueno, mi amor*, I'll be home very late." He lets me go to pull out and stuff himself back into his pants.

I'm about to bend over and pull up my pants, but he stops me and pushes me forward again. "*No te muevas*, don't move," he demands. He steps back, and, over my shoulder, I can see him watching me, his gaze moving down to my ass and exposed pussy.

His cum slowly starts leaking from my cunt, and a satisfied smirk crosses his face. He steps forward and shoves two fingers inside of me.

"You didn't come for me, Katherine." He strokes me and asks, "Why were you in here, Katherine?"

Fuck, he said my name twice.

"The security PIN didn't work this morning, so I came to ask if they changed it," I pant through each word, knowing he's not done with me yet.

"Hmmm." His fingers trail down to my clit and starts rubbing it painfully hard. "You aren't lying, are you, Katherine?" Matias doesn't let up, and I'm about to come when he stops rubbing my clit but continues stroking my pussy, excruciatingly slow.

My forehead hits the wall. "No, Matias, I came in and the alarm from the kitchen wouldn't set."

His pace quickens and I groan out loud. God, I need the release. He rubs my clit with our mixed juices again and I push back against his hand. My body tightens and, finally, I come on his hand and moan out with every touch. My breaths come out uneven and labored from the adrenaline rush I got from the release.

Matias gently strokes me, almost reverently, before saying, "My pretty little *puta*." He chuckles at me and then removes his hand, pulling my pants up before warning me, "I don't want to see your tits out again, *mi amor*."

He leaves me half-dressed and gutted in the hallway. If looks could kill, I would have murdered that motherfucker in that moment. All I could think of was throwing the knife from my boot into his retreating back.

CHAPTER 7

Tank
Las Vegas

Summertime in Vegas is no joke. You become a vampire and are out only from the evening to the early morning, sleeping all day to beat the heat. Which worked out great for us, most of our jobs being at night anyway.

I'm pretty sure I passed out on the couch instead of my room. My neck and back hurt like a motherfucker. My right arm is numb from something heavy. I crack an eye open just enough to see a red bandana.

A throat clearing above me startles me to find a grinning Maddox. "Not how I pictured my son and you would end up, sweetly snoring in each other's arms."

I start to sit up and push Axl's head away from me. "Get up, Axl." I look down at my bare chest that has a fresh tattoo across it. "Est 1983." Fuck, vague memories of Blade giving me this fresh tatt start to surface.

He jolts awake, "What the fuck..." Jumping up, he runs his hands over his face.

"You were cuddling me in the clubhouse, dude. No one was supposed to know about us, you promised me," I mildly shout out my fake astonishment.

"Shut the fuck up. I passed out and you take up the whole damn couch with your big ass body. Your stupid ass isn't my type."

"I know, you're holding out for your perfect little princess that loves Guns N' Roses as much as you. The perfect little sinner in all the land. A biker fairytale, so freakin' sweet." I hold my hands up under my chin, because his obsession never gets old.

A yawn stops me from further conversation. I lean forward and pour out a line of coke, and then one more. Holding one finger over one nostril and then a straw to the other, I huff up a fat line into my nose and cough at the dry white powder that coats the back of my throat.

"Zombie dust?" I pass Axl the mirror with coke on it. He does the same as me and takes a hit off our wake-up call. He finally notices my new chest piece and his eyes raise in question. I chug from the vodka bottle sitting in front of me and check my watch that says it is three in the afternoon. Fuck, what time did we pass out? Six in the morning, I think.

"I know, I'm still putting together last night too. I think Blade did it—"

My thoughts trail off as I catch Harley walking across the room and into the kitchen. Axl jumps up from the couch to follow her and ignores my comment, I'm sure to ask her to make his prissy ass breakfast. A heavy boot slams into my shin and pain follows.

"Quit eye fucking my woman, Tank. She's been out of your league for years," Maddox warns but there's some laughter in his voice.

I rub my shin, "I will try, but, Mad, you know she is hot."

"I'm not fucking stupid, kid. She wears my patch and ring for a reason. She. Is. Mine."

"Jesus, now I know where Axl gets his crazy 'all mine' from."

"It ain't crazy, you take care of what's yours and make no damn apology for it. That's why we work hard to keep everyone safe."

"Don't worry, I will take care of her should anything happen," I exaggerate with a few winks.

"If there was ever something to happen to me, you know that Axl will kill you himself if you thought about touching his mom."

"Fuck, ain't that the truth. I promise you, Mad Dog, I will look out for her."

"Careful, asshole, you almost sound like a man. Only if you assholes would stop snorting that shit. Tank, I'm telling you, you ain't gonna find nothing but bullshit at the end of that high. Find a woman that fucks you so hard, it gives you the same rush. You don't need that easy pussy and blow."

Maddox walks away shouting out, "Besides, Harley and I can't even hang out around the clubhouse because you little shits constantly have your little pricks out." He leaves me with a head full of advice. Fuck, I've got plenty of time to get my shit together.

After some food, coffee and a shower, I get my ass into the garage and look over the work orders, planning out who's doing what for the day.

I'm fucking sweating up a storm so I tear off my wife beater and finish torqueing down a bolt. A small finger runs over my back and lips touch the shell of my ear.

"Hey, baby," Ava purrs.

Huh, she clearly didn't get my brush off from last night. She wants more. I'll show her what it's like to be club pussy.

"What's up, Ava, are you looking to fuck?"

"Yes," she hisses and scrapes a nail down my back.

"Come back at eleven, I've got shit to do until then."

She plays off a coy smile and sways her hips for show on her way out. Bitch thinks she is gonna have it easy with me? The door shuts behind her and Axl frowns at me from the other side of the garage. "Do you think having her hang around here is a good idea?"

"Most definitely fucking not a good idea, but, don't worry, I have a plan."

"This should be a good one then," he chuckles from across the room.

"Oh, just wait." And I spend the rest of the day fantasizing about how epic I will make it stick in her head that she's not mine and never will be.

After some long hours, we finally finish up the work order for the day and I head to prepare for the night. Coke, weed, beer and shots line up the bar. All of it is ready except for the small bag of ecstasy in my pocket. These bitches are in for a treat tonight.

The brothers start pouring in along with the club pussy. Before long, the music is loud, and coke starts being snorted, or licked, off pussy and asses.

I start making my rounds, offering any willing girls wanting an extra hit of pleasure some X for the evening. More than half of them are down for just about anything, and that is some exciting shit to watch.

Trix walks in topless and I call her over, grabbing a handful of her ass. "I need you to stay by my side for a bit, sexy."

She answers by grabbing my dick in turn, humming and sucking on my neck. I hold up the ecstasy in front of her face and she holds her mouth open. Trix chugs down the pill with the beer from my hand and latches onto me.

Blade walks in and his eyes flare a bit as he's taking in the scene, with Spider right behind him. He heads straight over to me. "Why is there a giant orgy breaking out? Fuck, bro, it's too early for this shit."

"I handed out X to make a point, you'll see why here in a few."

Blade scrutinizes me for a moment, and, of course, Spider does too, then they relax enough to watch the live porn that has broken out. It doesn't take Trix long to start grinding all over me and have my bare ass in a chair in the middle of the room.

She grabs a condom and caresses my cock while she covers my dick in latex. I groan and toss my head back when she straddles the chair and sits herself onto my dick. She grinds down and moans out.

My head comes up and I find another club girl staring at us from across the room as Trix and I are fucking. I wave her over and she joins us hurriedly, ready to make us a threesome of everyone's fantasy.

"Turn around, Trix."

She does as I ordered and sits back down on my cock with her pussy on full display for the crowd.

"Eat her pussy, bitch," I grind out, sounding much harsher than I intended, but my balls are about to explode.

The club slut gets onto her knees and strokes over Trixie's pussy. She shudders and I pull her back to rest on my chest as I scoot forward on the chair. Trixie brings up her feet to rest them on my knees.

The bitch on the floor latches onto my balls with her mouth first and licks up what is exposed of my dick all the way to Trixie's clit. I pull and twist her nipples as we both get the bitch's mouth.

That's the moment when the prospect walks Ava in as I ordered him to do earlier after she left. She stands there in front of me, stunned, with wide eyes.

"Get behind the bitch on the floor and get your fingers in her cunt or get the fuck out and never come back here."

Ava blinks and her nose twitches before a single tear falls and she rips out of the clubhouse like her ass is on fire. Safe to say, I will never see her lying, cheating ass ever again.

The night caries on and I have never seen so many orgasms in one night. Also, I have never been given that many high fives from the brothers in one night. Except, the next morning when my head is pounding from the massive hangover in my head.

Some may think that I got my road my name because I'm a big motherfucker, and, while that holds true, I also am known for the biggest fucking parties, and am responsible for the 'tank' that parked itself inside your head the morning after. The 'tank of a hangover'.

"Tank," Stryker bellows at me at our early morning church. His baritone voice makes me wince. "That fucking bullshit that happened last night will never happen again. Fucking acting like teenagers."

He points a meaty finger and glares at me until I confirm with a response.

"Aye, Prez, it shouldn't be a problem," I finish with a serious face. I almost lose it when Spider grins at me. Fucker wants me to lose it and laugh because then Stryker will put a fist through my face for laughing at him.

Clearing my throat, I erase my thoughts and focus back onto the meeting.

Traitors deserve only one thing, retribution and paybacks.

CHAPTER 8

Matias

Fucking Katherine was up to no good in there. But I'll let her have her secrets for now. I slide back into the car and Esteban gives me a once over. I glare back at him and Angel. Esteban knows why I insisted on coming home. I could give a fuck. I do or fuck what and who I want, *when* I want.

I pull out my phone and look over the missed calls, then instruct the driver to take us to my father's office.

The three of us enter the tall building that's housing my father's offices in downtown Mexico City. We walk past the receptionist and she smiles sweetly at us, wishing one of us would throw her a pity fuck. No way am I fucking my father's leftovers.

I rap my knuckles on the door before stepping into the office, not waiting for him to give us permission to do so. My father's annoyed face looks up at us as Angel and I take a seat, while Esteban shuts the door behind him.

"Did you set Cobra straight? We can't run these bitches through California any longer. The Feds are onto us already," he barks his demands at us.

"*Sí*, Padre, we talked to him. He knows he needs to make it happen, or Katherine dies. He's going to make it happen or take control of the area. We will work it out."

My father is a *pendejo* to believe that Cobra gives a fuck about his daughter other than to use her as leverage. If he needed her to die, he would be the first to put a bullet in her head. He sure as fuck doesn't worry about losing her.

I sigh. This is going to take a while, and I'd rather not deal with him before the drop in a few hours. Either my father or Cobra will die before *she* does. I'm working on several plans to make sure that won't happen. Only Angel, my brother, knows of them.

"*Bueno*, and moving the *drogas*, drugs, up north?" he questions with a raised brow.

"We are setting up a hit on the Battle Born MC and hijacking a truck that pays for their runs through their territory to make it look like Cobra's crew is involved. Battle Born cannot have a reputation when it comes to hijacking on their turf."

Taking a breath, I look out the window. "Stryker, their president, must go after Cobra. Cobra can't get the MC over there to cooperate so we will slowly infiltrate the U.S. turf from the north and get our services moving."

This is all so simple, and, while my good old father is busy with these details, I have other matters to see to.

Angel sits forward and forcefully keeps his voice level. "What about the daughter of Cuervo? You promised me a marriage for alliances." Whatever his addiction to this woman is, it has made him weak.

"No," our father simply states. "She is of no use to us and hasn't been for a long time. Cuervo could have become something bigger within the club, but he's not worth much to their crew to bargain a marriage for."

My father doesn't notice but I do see the tic in Angel's jaw and the twitch in his hands. My eyes don't leave him until he notices me looking, and he sees that now is not the time, but soon. This American pussy is how I will control Angel to get what I want. I give him a faint nod, and, slowly, he slides back into his seat.

"Get back to work," my father, the Cartel boss, *The King*, demands. "Meet up with Cobra at the warehouse and make sure the women are shipped out to the next drop. Cobra is taking the drugs and diamonds back up with him."

I signal over for Angel to get up. "No worries, father, Angel and I have this under control." He stands with me and I clap him on the back, giving him false hopes.

Together, the three of us leave his office to start the ball rolling. I need to go speak with a few contacts in Las Vegas. I pull the phone from my pocket and dial.

"Diego," I greet the man when he answers, "we have a task for you. Clean up a truck moving north on highway ninety-five."

"I'll switch patrol areas. What time is this truck coming through, and what do I do with the merchandise?"

"Hold it for now. Angel will be up eventually to check on the area, and he'll pick it up then with a crew." I pause for a moment. "Get familiar with the Battle Born MC, in particular their one member, John Smith, alias is Crank."

I hang up the call and tap the phone against my chin on our drive to the warehouse to meet with Cobra. I plan the angles to make this work, double checking that I'm not missing anything.

The streets pass in a blur and I lose track of where we are. We stop abruptly, jarring me from my thoughts. Esteban gets out of the car first and checks the location along with the men from two other armed black cars that escorted us here. Dirty fucking bikers are only useful for transporting the shit the rest of us don't have time for, but we still need to be careful and not let our guard down.

The sun is starting to set, the windows glaring with the reflection of the bright rays. Dust particles become visible, cloaking the warehouse. I pull my shades from my suit pocket and shield my eyes putting them on. I step in front of Esteban, he and Angel following behind, watching my back. Together, the three of us walk over to Cobra and the rest of his MC, patiently waiting for the report on his shipment.

"The brothers pulled in a variety, from young to matured, and a few younger *niños* as your handlers requested in inventory. They are waiting in the truck." Cobra, the smug bastard, smirks.

It's fucking disgusting knowing that these assholes fucked every last one of them on the way down here. Even I have some fucking standards of who I fuck.

"Open," I bark at him.

One of his men pop the latch and lifts the heavy panel. The stench reaches me from twenty feet away. I don't move or flinch from the disgusting smell of urine and shit. Not my concern, and I don't care as long as the shipment makes it to its destination unharmed. I lift a hand to Angel, and he passes the bag with cash over to Cobra.

"When are we moving the drugs through the States? I want an estimated time of arrival for the drop."

Cobra's eyes squint ever so slightly before I add, "Sensitive shit in this one. Not your fucking concern other than to do your job, like I pay you to do."

"We leave tomorrow afternoon, can't before then. My guy working the border will be there at the time set. It will take us a few days to get up north. I'll keep you updated."

"*Bueno*, take the gray shipment truck." Cobra lifts his chin and I nod in goodbye before turning to leave.

It seems that Cobra has his own agenda in Mexico City, and that makes it my fucking business. But to have Cobra stall half a day is actually perfect.

"Angel, fly up to Reno, Nevada, immediately and set up there, then wait for my instructions while I handle everything here. Create distractions only as I instruct."

I pause because I know what he is going to do, he'll find Jennifer, the woman that was promised to him by my father that he refuses to allow him to have now. I should feel guilty, but I don't.

"Also, go pay off that lawyer up there to infiltrate and work with that MC of Battle Born. We need the transport access. Make it happen, and, when we take over the MC, you can have your precious American *puta*."

I would feel sorry for the fucking bitch, except she is exactly what I need to reel Angel in. He is my brother after all, and if he doesn't eventually get what he wants, he will kill me too.

CHAPTER 9

Tank
Las Vegas, about three years ago...

Stryker bellows from the hall for us to get to church. After the men gather and the door shuts, a very pissed off Prez, looks at us all before telling us why we are here.

"It's suspected that there are a few trucks moving across our territory and not paying for access through Nevada." He stops to let out an exhale. "From what I know of the increase in trucks and with Cobra constantly on my ass to allow him transport, I suspect he knows who they belong to and wants back into our good graces."

Maddox, the VP, holds up a hand. "That isn't going to go down well with Fuego and his crew up north."

Stryker nods, "I know, and I feel it in my gut that someone is setting up to take us over."

I can't say I'm surprised by this because of the past feud, but what we all can guarantee is one thing. It is about to get a whole lot worse before this will get any better.

"Crank, you and Tank hit the freeway and have first watch. Split up into teams and I'll text out a schedule. Until then, no fucking booze, bitches or blow," Stryker orders us and slams down the gavel. Church is over but I have a long night with Crank watching the road.

As we filter out, I catch up to Blade and Axl. "He said the B's of life, brothers, booze, bitches and blow." Blade shakes his head at me and Axl laughs, "I want some head before I head to bed, another fucking B."

Even though I feel that today will turn into a shit day, I try to keep it light and joke, move forward or else the stress could eat us alive.

Crank and I suit up for the ride out. We don't wear our cuts or take our bikes but instead hit the highway in a black truck.

For hours, we call in trucks and van plates until we get lucky. We find an unregistered truck that hasn't reported to the club and we follow him. Almost too easy to be true and my instincts flare up.

"Crank, I think this fucker wants us to follow him. Ease up, brother, and let me put in a call to Stryker first."

"Don't be a fucking pussy, Tank." Crank, the old bastard, snarls at me. I hold my hands up for a moment. But, fuck this asshole, and decide to send off a text to Stryker anyway, letting him know where we are and what we found.

The cargo truck takes a turn off the freeway into an industrial area outside the city. He parks the truck and starts getting out. *Fuck!* I internally scream before I see

Stryker texting back, saying to keep our asses where they are until he gets here.

Crank takes off through the buildings, not waiting for me as his backup. Gunfire goes off into the short distance and I run up, holding my gun out in front of me while firing at the cargo truck that's hauling off.

Crank holds his chest and spits up blood. "Fucking Cobra had his man transporting, tell Stryker." He spits up more blood.

Holstering my gun, I rip off my shirt and hold it to his chest. It feels useless with the amount of blood that now has saturated the fabric. Two shots in each lung, fuck. He's done.

I stand up and roar out the frustration of the whole thing. If the stupid bastard listened, he would still be breathing. Pulling out my phone, I call Stryker and inform him that we need a clean-up van now too.

By the time that he and the club make it to where we are, fire has lightened up the club and Styker wants revenge. He, Maddox and Titan take off after the man I described in the truck. The other one, I have never seen, and, as much as I tried to slow them down, revenge was the only thing they understood.

I help with loading Crank into the van to bury him on an unmarked grave out in the desert. Like this shit couldn't get any worse, but no bodies, no evidence, and, unfortunately, Crank just became evidence. His body is removed of anything that could identify him, like his wallet and cut which Spider bags and throws into the truck. His club tatt is burned away with a torch.

A coyote howls off into the distance and an eerie feeling surrounds us, rendering us all silent before Blade looks up at the sky. "Stryker found him, he's dead." Axl, Spider and I look at each other for clarity, but words are left unsaid.

A grave is dug with shovels and four men into to the early morning sunset. Crank is lowered inside before he is covered, and we all stand speechless, in our own way saying goodbye to a member.

None of us has ever had to bury a man. This is a day not a one of us will ever forget. The reality. Nothing lasts forever, bet on today and not tomorrow.

This is the moment when the four us become men of the Battle Born. The day we buried one of our own is the day when life and death gets tattooed into our souls.

You are not born until you battle.

Battle Born.

CHAPTER 10

Katherine

Maria, our housekeeper, keeps looking at me over the stove while she cleans the kitchen.

"I need your help today." I decide to shoot her straight. If there is any way to get her help, I have to be blunt with her.

"*Para qué*? For what?"

Stepping closer to her, I lay a hand on her shoulder, hoping to gain her sympathy. "I need to see *mi papa* before he leaves, and Matias, I'm scared to ask him." I clam up and look down at the floor.

Maria huffs out a breath, "*Mija*, your husband will kill me. Literally." She gives me a pointed look and I know she's right.

"I know he won't be happy. I'll just tell him I took you to lunch and my father showed up," I plead with her. She shakes her head, and I know that I won.

"We leave to get supplies for the house, and you came to the bakery to gather groceries, *sí*?"

"*Sí*, Maria, *gracias*."

After we both are ready to leave, I notify Maria and she distracts the guards with *sopaipillas* while I dart and lie down in the back of her car. She opens and shuts the door before muttering, "This is so silly, *mija*, really."

The guards watch her, and she hollers out, "*Adiós*," waving as she drives out.

When we pull up to the small store, I ask her, "Do you recognize anyone? Did anyone follow us?"

She looks around and grabs her bag, then looks behind us. "No. Be back here in thirty minutes, *no más*." She gets out of the car, and, a few moments after her, I do the same. My breathing gets labored as I quickly walk the three blocks, dodging hundreds of people before I reach my father who is sitting at a table.

"Nice hat and sunglasses," he chuckles at me.

"Do you want to be shot for eating with me?" I deadpan.

He stops laughing and leans forward. "Take the bag next to me, it will have everything you need. Follow your instruction as you were taught." He leans in a little closer. "Matias has something planned, I need you to find out what and let me know. He tried to have me followed today." He gets up from the table. "Keep your eyes and ears open," he advises before turning to leave.

"I need information on a guard, Juan Cervantes, as soon as possible," I manage to squeeze out before he's out of here with a nod of acknowledgement.

Quickly, I grab the bag and take it with me out of the busy restaurant, then hurry to meet Maria. I barely make it back right before she does. She looks down at me, then buckles up and leaves the city to head back to the house.

I feel safe, for now at least, but it saddens me what I have to do next. I take the phone out and text Cobra. Maria needs to be taken care of.

A moment later, I know when I receive a text back that it is done. I close my eyes and push the pain away, knowing the monster that created the evil in this world lives within me too.

As soon as I get into my room, I stuff the cash, phone and Glock in plastic bags. Then, I clip the bags to shirt hangers and cover them with my suit jackets and shirt sets.

While I wait for Matias to get home, I strategize his possible next move. This cat and mouse game is growing intense.

To keep the appearances, I start dinner for us and set out the food on the counter for shrimp fajitas. I glance up when Korina walks in. She looks hesitant to be in the same room as me.

"What were you doing today? I came by and no one knew that you weren't here, Katherine. Does Matias know you were gone?" She tosses her bag down after firing her questions and squares up to me with her hands on her hips.

"I went out to buy my husband our favorite dinner, Korina. What I do or don't do is none of your business anyway, or is it?"

She glares at me and swallows, not sure what else to say to me. "He is going to find out you weren't here."

I jerk my head in confusion. "Korina, is there something wrong with surprising him? Please don't ruin it for me." *Or, I may have to stab you with a kitchen knife.* I don't add that, but I know without a doubt that I'm not the one who will die today.

"I do appreciate your thoughts and concern, I was just so happy to make this for him for our anniversary," I explain with as much fake enthusiasm as I can muster. "So, you said you came by looking for me then? For what?"

The surprise on her face is like a slap to the face. Stunned, she stands there speechless. I wave a hand at her, "Oh man, you have it bad for Esteban, don't you?" I tease. "I can't wait to tell Matias, he will be so happy to hear this!"

"NO, please," she stumbles forward. "He–uh, doesn't want anyone to know yet. We haven't, um, we will soon, okay?"

"Don't wait too long, okay? Your secret is safe with me like I know mine is with you, right?" The little *pinche perra* grabs her bag and fakes a laugh, waving me goodbye.

"Sure is." She walks out, leaving me and forgetting all about the fucking knife she left in my back.

Soon after she leaves, Matias is strolling in with a pleased look on his face, sitting down at the table. I grab a Corona and his plate, then walk over, softly placing the food and beer down in front of him. His hand darts out and captures my wrist in a tight grip.

"Katherine." He scoots his chair back and pulls me down in his lap. "Happy anniversary, *mi amor.*"

My heart is pounding in my ears. I just never know what his actions really mean. I slowly raise my hand and cup his cheek. "Happy anniversary," I repeat the words back that taste like vomit in my mouth.

Matias' hand comes up and runs over the protruding, pounding vein in my neck, running his thumb over it.

"What is it, Katherine?" he whispers and kisses along the vein, then licks it with a long moan.

"You." It is a confession, but I don't add how much I despise him and how hard my heart is pounding from fear.

"Mmm," he responds and cups my tits before removing my shirt and then my bra. "Stand," he commands, and I do listen, for now.

Slowly, Matias pulls my pants down my legs and removes them, followed by his own. His strong hands pull me back forward but this time he has me straddle his dick.

"Fuck me, Katherine, make me come in this pussy that belongs to me."

Everything in my body screams at me to run, but I don't, and I do as he asks, and I fuck my husband, on a chair, in our kitchen, on our tenth wedding anniversary.

Matias rocks me back and forth by my hips, grinding me down hard while he shoots his release into me. "Fuck, I don't want you to move. I want my cum to stay inside you."

I close my eyes and lean forward, concealing my shock from him. Oh my God, why would he want that? Only one thing comes to mind and this just got that much worse. I hold on to him, terrified and too frozen to move in my panicked state. His fingers trail up and down my spine.

"I need you, Katherine, I need you to talk to your father and get close to him. Would you do that for me?"

Nausea rolls through my body in waves, because now he just turned me into Korina.

A little snitch in his game of lies.

CHAPTER 11

Matias

"What the fuck do you mean Maria is dead?" I snarl into the phone.

Esteban sighs at the other end. "Cops just called. It was a mugging gone wrong. They took her phone, purse, jewelry and car. She was left with a cut throat in a ditch. Fuck." Someone interrupts him before he comes back to me. "Her last call was to your burner phone. The call was missed at the time of her death."

The employees are only allowed to dial that number under extreme circumstances.

"I don't think it was a random. If she was killed while getting mugged, they would have taken her by surprise. She was targeted. Find out why, Esteban, we don't need any distractions from tonight or tomorrow." I disconnect the call and curl my body back into Katherine's where she lies on her side with her back to me.

My fingers trail over her silky skin, from her hip to her shoulder, then I lightly drag her hair away from her face. "You're awake, *mi amor*." My lips press a kiss to her shoulder and my hand runs down her body where I hold her still flat stomach.

"Yes," she croaks out and clears her throat.

"I need you to rest, it's barely dawn. Sleep in. I need to go meet Esteban." I don't really need to explain, she was lying next to me when I took the call, and heard me.

I need her pregnant with my child as soon as possible. And, with the amount of times I've fucked her over the last few months and then again last night, it's a real possibility.

Katherine

Cobra. I knew that he would kill Maria, and, from the sounds of it, it was barely in time before she ratted me out to Matias. That was too close. I need to be more careful if I want to make it out alive.

My stomach starts turning again, but this time I believe it is because of my guilt for my hand in getting a good woman killed.

A part of me believes that, except, she was paid well to work for Matias, knowing the possible consequences, just like I do. I can die at any given moment. I'm wrapping myself up in these lies, and, if I'm not careful, I'll be caught in my own web.

Pulling myself up, my weak body protests at leaving the warm bed, and I slowly walk into the bathroom. At the sink, I splash cool water on my face.

In my mind, I pray for the guilt or nausea to leave, but neither does. The nausea increases, and, a second later, I race to the toilet before my vomit can hit the floor.

I empty whatever was in my stomach in seconds, with a gut-wrenching force. A sickness I've never felt in my life overcomes me.

And, just like that, the game has changed, and I must leave before he realizes what I have of value to him.

I am pregnant with a Cartel prince.

My hand trembles as I wipe my mouth. No, this can't be happening now.

A cold sweat breaks out over my forehead. My forearm wipes it away but the worry intensifies. How could this be? I *know* that I had my shot a few months ago. I've been so careful about it in the last couple of years.

My body rests as I sit down next to the toilet, with my back to the wall, and I allow myself to cry for a few moments. I can only feel pain. A pain so deep that it shatters me in two. My husband betrayed me one last time. It's the only thing that makes sense.

Tears stream down my face, and I breathe through it all like they are drops of betrayal leaving me with every single splash down my chest. I am being swallowed up by the grief, and I let it take me for the ride, allowing it to crash into me with the force of a hurricane.

My father and Matias are both going to kill me when they discover what I have done, and all this will come crashing down. But, one thing I know with clarity. They can't have my baby. He is mine.

Pure will and determination drives me to get up and get back into the fight and finish this. My heart strengthens and the tears stop. I walk over to the mirrors and look at myself, Katherine, the wife of one of the biggest kingpins in Mexico, a Cartel Prince himself. I promise my baby to never cry again, to be stronger than anything or anyone that I have ever seen.

There is only one reason Matias would want me knocked up. To secure himself with his father, *El Rey*, the King himself. I also wonder what my father has done, because it is clear that I am of no use to the Cartel boss. The puzzle starts snapping together, one piece at a time. Something big is going down today with Cobra and Matias and the Battle Born MC.

Cobra does all their transport in the U.S. and that MC in Nevada controls the western border. My father has failed them in some way, and I am of no use to hold over him anymore. But I don't think that is all.

I step into the shower and rinse away the toxic feelings, breathing strength in along with the hot mist. If there was ever a right time to escape, today would be that day. I can feel it deep within my bones.

After I am cleaned up and dressed, I go back into the closet and pull my burner phone out to call Cobra.

"Papa," I wait a second for him to acknowledge me, the background growing quiet and I hear a door shutting closed.

"Katherine, what do you have for me?"

"Matias knows that Maria is dead because she tried to call him right before one of your men killed her. We are fucked, they are going to kill us over this. I need to leave now."

He hesitates before growling at me, "You keep your *puta* ass there and do as you're told. I need to know his next move."

My mind jumps back and forth over everything that I heard or read in the last few days, a map of the Battle Born territory and the date for today. Matias is planning on taking them all down today.

I steel my nerves and respond like the perfect little soldier he wants to sacrifice for his greed. "*Sí*, Papa. Were you able to find any dirt on the man I asked about the other day, Juan Cervantes?"

"He gambles and owes a debt for cock fighting. Also, he has a thing for young girls. You want proof?

Send me something fucking useful on your husband, and I'll email it to the account on your phone."

"I'll be in touch," I say softly and hang up the call, hoping like hell that part of Matias' plan is to kill the son of a bitch. I power off the phone and tuck it with the other stuff that I had hidden away.

I pull out every black piece of clothing that I have and pack it all into a backpack along with the credit card and knife that I stole from the security guard. Matias has several handguns hidden around the house and I pluck a couple from the lesser obvious locations, leaving mine in my nightstand, as usual.

I take all the supplies that I packed in the bag with me to Matias' office where I grab the papers that I printed the other day, tucking them into the bag as well. I sit down at his desk and stare at the closed laptop, knowing that I have about three password attempts before I'm locked out, and about three minutes to get what I need from his laptop once I do log in, if I even manage to do it at all. I find a thumb drive and flip it around in my hand, steeling my nerves for what I'm about to do.

A few deep breaths go in and a few deep breaths come out. I look around his office for a clue as to what his password could be. Maybe it's my name? I highly doubt it. What is he more in love with than me... His money, and greed, and power.

While I think about it, I rip a small piece of tape and paper off a notebook he has on his desk. Barely opening the laptop, I cover the camera before opening the device the rest of the way.

I power the machine on and stare at it. Three guesses, that's all I get. Matias means "gift of God". Okay, my second guess would be, "money is power," and, my last guess... Shit, could it be my name after all? I can't think of anything else. Fuck.

I quickly stick in the thumb drive and then type in the first password I came up with. *Failed Attempt* pops up in red. "Shit!" I whisper shout and try again. My heart is pounding from the adrenaline when I type the second one and fail again.

My hands are shaking in fear. I look again across the room at a picture that has words scrolled across. It says "*Reyes Malditos*, Cursed Kings have all the riches but no souls". I quickly type in just *Reyes Malditos*. And I'm in.

My fingers fly over the keys and click on any and every doc I can find. I save everything while I keep an eye on the clock.

Movement catches my eye in the hallway. I rip the thumb drive out and stuff it into my bag, peeling the piece of paper off the camera and turning the laptop off just before closing it shut. Korina calls my name and walks into the office.

Matias sent her as a distraction, I'm sure, until he could get here himself, to keep me talking and distracted. She doesn't live far from the house, so it's not a surprise.

I start thinking of all the visits and shopping trips we went on together. Was she ever my sister and a friend? I smile at her now, acting as if her presence is completely normal, and pick up my bag.

"Morning, sister."

She hesitates at the door with a scowl on her face. "I'll be happy when he kills you, maybe then he will let me be free!" she screeches, not willing to hold back anymore.

"It was never my fault for what he did to you, Korina." I shoulder pass her and she follows me through the house.

"No, but every single person in our lives always chooses you over me."

The bitterness in her voice is alarming. In the last few weeks she's grown into someone I didn't realize she had become. My enemy.

"That's not true, what about Esteban? Does he know you fuck his boss, too?" I question, because, really, who the fuck does *she* think she is, acting all innocent. "*You* chose Matias over me, Korina."

I stop for just a moment and turn to look at her. "Come with me, we'll escape this together," I try one last time, just to see if there is possibly any ounce of the old Korina left buried under all this hate.

"Everything has been *your* fault for a long time. I grew to hate you for pulling me into all of this. At first, I loved him too, you know, Matias, then I learned what I was to him, a puppet in his game to get to you. Just like Papa, he uses me to control you. I hate you. I hate that even though you look like me, you are always the better one."

She pants out a breath and finally takes her last dig at me. "I was there when Papa killed Mama. He killed her because she was trying to protect *you* from him. He shot her in the head with no tears in his eyes because of *you*. She was going to run away with *you*, and he caught her."

Her icy glare penetrates my soul, but I don't even have time to think her words over. "I'll praise the moment when you stop breathing on the same earth as me, and I'll tell Papa or Matias whatever I need to in order to make that finally happen." She looks down at the bag in my hand and then back up into my eyes.

Hate spreads deep in my heart like the veins of poison she injected me with. I despise this life and her for spewing her venom at me for it all when all I ever did was try to protect her.

"Hmmm," I decide to play with her. "What will Matias *do* when he finds out you've been fucking Esteban?" I ask, tilting my head to the side. "If you want to play this game, Korina, you will lose."

I set the bag down at my side and take two steps to stand in front of her.

"The fucking my husband part, I get, because I know the devil himself, and *that* I could forgive. The plotting behind my back, *that* I cannot."

She looks away, then up at the windows, and I know I'm out of time. I grip the long and thick gold chain necklace from around her neck tightly and maneuver myself behind her. Then I pull it back as hard as I can while she struggles. She scratches at my arms and kicks at my feet before falling to the floor. I pull up and quickly slam her head down, hard, onto the tile floor. My arms and hands are on fire from her claw marks.

She lies there, lifeless, with blood pouring from her nose. It was either her or the child I'm carrying, and besides, she was waiting for them to come and kill me.

I grab the backpack and toss it over my shoulder while I wait around a corner. I count down slowly to calm my nerves, like I was taught. Two guards come running in through the foyer, yelling and screaming at seeing Korina lying ghastly still on the white tile floor. I pull the nine-millimeter from my back and aim with both hands on the handle, steady, straight arms. I set one in my sights and send a bullet into his skull.

The other guard whips his head up, and, just as he spots me and begins to raise his gun, I pull the trigger and hit his shoulder first and then pop two more bullets into his lungs.

I don't dare to move. I take in deep breaths and listen while the chaos settles. Walking up a little closer, I keep my ears observant over the gurgling noise from the one guard I shot in the lungs.

I pick up their tossed guns and run down the hallway with adrenaline flooding my veins. I reach the car that's parked in the garage and toss in the bag through the passenger seat, then jump in, starting the engine. The garage door creeps open, and I pray to the heavens up above that there aren't any armed men waiting for me on the other side.

Putting the car into Drive, I steadily move forward, looking around for any traps. When I don't see any, I gun it as fast as I can down the long driveway, nearly hitting another vehicle when I emerge into traffic.

At the nearest busy street, I park the car, leaving the engine running. I hope to God that someone takes off in it. The GPS will keep them looking for a few hours. I walk inside a building and then straight back out through the side entrance and down the alleyways.

I walk for blocks until I come across a bus station and hop on. I take as many busses as possible to get across the large city before nightfall. I purchase a hat from a vendor on a street and go into an electronic store to purchase a cheap laptop. I pay the cashier with Juan Cervantes' credit card which I then drop on the floor in the store, once again hoping that someone will pick it up and use it.

The sun is setting already which means that every moment that passes at this point is critical.

Every breath I take, a gift.

CHAPTER 12

Matias

"What the fuck do you mean *she got away*?" I roar into the phone at one of the men that arrived minutes after she left. He sends me pictures of the dead bodies on the floor and explains to me that Katherine, *my wife*, is nowhere to be found. Today of all days she pulls this shit on me. "Keep looking for her and tell no one."

I disconnect the call and fight the urge to run after her, find her and choke her myself.

There was too much at stake with the business when I got the call that someone logged into my laptop at home. I knew it was her right away, and that shit surprised me. It changed everything between us in ways I don't even understand. Why now?

I pull my thoughts together and get back to work, placing a call to our contact over in Las Vegas. After I finish business, I am going after her, and she will regret the day she betrayed me and our marriage.

"What's the update? Did you get the cargo truck that Cobra's men were hauling?"

"*Sí*, the truck is stored and ready for Angel when he gets down here."

"I'll transfer the money as soon as the second part is done, like we discussed. Two bodies are to be found, one Battle Born and one of Cobra's men, *sí*?"

Done with him, I hang up and call Cobra. "*Hola*, Cobra, we have a fucking problem, *pendejo*, *mis drogas* are missing at the drop. I made it pretty fucking clear that we had a deadline to meet, not to mention millions of dollars are fucking missing in drugs and diamonds."

Cobra's deadly silent. "What the fuck!" he then roars into my ear.

"The *pinche policía* I pay off to monitor the roads said that he thinks Battle Born was hauling my truck up there, but it never showed up," I inform him calmly.

"Stryker, that motherfucker, wouldn't be so stupid," he growls back.

"You better get this shit handled before I get up there, Cobra," I warn and tap off the phone, then wait.

Shortly after, my father, the seventy-year-old man, comes in, sweating bullets. "*Que pasó*, if we don't get that truck up north, this…" He trails off, knowing the implications of what this looks like among his associates. He guaranteed them the transport in that area. It looks as if he stole his own cargo to rip off the men who had already payed for it.

Soon, we are surrounded by the many men we contract with, very displeased with my father, the

Cartel boss, who looks like a liar and a cheat, all because *I* have been lying to him. He turns to me and doesn't say a word because the damage is done. And he knows it.

I would like to think there is some pride in his eyes when he realizes the way I'm about to take over his empire. It is, after all, an honorable death to have your son mercifully put the bullet in between your eyes and take what's rightfully his, the throne to the Cartel.

We are merely a few feet away from each other. My hand grips the handgun and I point the barrel at his head, smiling right before I blow his brains out. The man who raised me and made me into what I am today lies on the floor in front of me. He stares up to the heavens with his eyes wide open.

Today, I become the boss and king. In this very moment, I feel unstoppable.

No turf wars, because his men have been my men. And it's all mine, except for the fact that my queen is missing.

I apologize to all the men and hand out large stacks of cash, promising them that I would settle this.

I sit in my office and act as if my home is not a mess with dead bodies lying around and Katherine still missing. I am rooted to the spot, never having felt the sting of betrayal like I have from her, unable to go home and not have her there waiting for me. Ten years, just gone.

I pour myself a drink while the sun sets, and wait for any word from her, but nothing by the time the sun comes back up. There's no sign of her, and a piece of me breaks at why she would do this to me. A part of me realizes the weakness in me for her, and the demon rises.

Fury overcomes me, so intense that even her death would not calm it. She fucking betrayed me after all I have done for her.

My phone goes off and I see that it's Cobra finally calling me back.

"Those fucking *gringos* stole the truck and killed my man. Stryker believes we killed his club member. It's a fucking mess, Matias. And we are going to war."

At least *this* has gone to plan. I am the boss of my own empire, but my queen is gone.

My greed has turned me into a cursed king.

CHAPTER 13

Tank

War.

The mother Battle Born chapter has declared a war on the Mexican MC. At least that is what Cobra thought when he found his man dead and being eaten alive by the animals in the desert. I'm secretly sad we didn't do it. Stryker found the truck, but the men were long gone.

We have, however, declared lockdown. All the women and children are locked up tight in the clubhouse while we load trucks with men and ammunition. Maddox is holding Harley to his chest, and I overhear him promising her that he would bring their son back home to her.

When he kisses her one last time, he whispers, "In this life and the next, baby." He leaves her standing alone, and the woman looks as though she could crumble.

The Ol' Lady of the house, Moxie, Stryker's woman, rushes over to keep her from falling apart. Her strength is unwavering, although, I bet that inside, she is shattered. But she holds her shit together for her man because she has a fucking job and she does it well. Moxie is a tough bitch, and pride like I've never felt swells my chest.

I walk over to Harley. "They both are coming the fuck home." Her teary eyes search mine as she sees my promise. I will die before they do.

We ride over to our meeting point into the desert, away from the border patrol where we find an impressive caravan set up before us of the *Los Reyes Malditos*, the Cursed Kings MC. Ice and Fuego also brought their men down.

Cuervo is standing off to the side like a crazed man, chomping at the bit to be let free. He is wielding two machetes in his hands, pacing back and forth behind Fuego, his brother as well as the Prez of the California chapter.

Out of all of us, Cuervo wants Cobra dead the most for killing his wife, years before. A debt that has been left unsettled between the two for a decade or more. A bloody and haunted past still paints the future red because of greed, drugs and betrayal.

Stryker yells out, "Save your men, Cobra, and step out in front of them. We only want your fucking head."

Cobra's menacing laugh echoes across the wind. "*Matarlos a todos.*"

"Kill them all!" Cuervo bellows, repeating him, then starts running at full speed, aiming for Cobra, but doesn't get far with all the men that stop him.

Fuego covers his brother with gunfire, shooting and killing any man that gets too close or points a gun in his direction. The Vice Presidents cover the Presidents and aim for any possible threats.

Gunfire lights up the darkening sky like fireworks along with screams from the dying, carried through the howling winds. Ghost, Fuego's VP, the creepy motherfucker, starts working from the shadows, veering off to the sidelines to gain a sniper's advantage.

I stick to Axl's side and cover him through the chaos and whizzing bullets that buzz past us. We aim and fire, and, as a team. Standing side by side, we walk forward, spraying bullets.

A man lying in the dirt lifts his hand and raises his gun to Blade. On reflex, I pull the trigger and shoot the man in the head before his shot goes off. Dust and smoke coat the air like fog, making it hard to see who's left.

Cuervo yells, "I'll kill you, *pinche pendejo*." We all turn towards the shouting as Cobra jumps into the van with the rest of his men that start to retreat. Being outnumbered from the beginning, they didn't stand much of a chance.

We take the few fallen men back with us right before leaving. We make a pile of Cobra's men and light them on fire with diesel fuel, then haul ass out of there before the Feds and their helicopter find us.

For the next week, it is blasted all over the news about the drug deal gone wrong, and how the Feds are still investigating, looking for suspects.

Ghost made a call into his military contacts before we left. No one is looking into shit; one less trafficker for the government to worry about. We should send them a bill for cleaning up these pieces of shit.

What's next is on all of our minds. How many more need to die before Cobra is the one to pay his debt?

CHAPTER 14

Katherine

On the dark streets in the slums of Mexico City, I am in search of a coyote. A man that will help transport me over the border, safely. It must be done now while Matias is busy with his war games and drugs. God only knows what else. It can't be any jump the boarder coyote either. I need someone to smuggle me over completely undetected.

Unfortunately for me, everyone knows who I am. My body has grown so tired. The only place I can think of where I could possibly be safe for a handful of hours is the hospital for which I saw a sign a few miles back.

After riding on yet another bus and thirty minutes later, I am walking the hospital hallways, looking for a room where I can lie down and catch a few hours of sleep.

While I'm wandering around, I come across a deserted desk. I snag a nurse's purse and the ID she had sitting on top. I walk some more and, as I pass carts that are outside patients' rooms, I grab syringes with needles and bottles, tucking everything away as I go. I get to the end of a hallway and find a secluded room where a man who looks to be asleep is hooked up to a bunch of monitors.

I sit in a chair next to the bed and tuck the backpack to my side, curling up next to it. My life is in this bag, and, if I lose it, I am as good as dead. I pass out not having another choice. My body is exhausted from the day I had, and the baby is wearing on me.

It feels like only minutes later that I hear whispers in the room. I open my eyes only to find two nurses talking to each other. They both turn and smile at me when they hear me moving. "Is he your husband?" one of them politely asks.

"No, I'm sorry, he is my boyfriend." I look to the floor like I am ashamed. "I know I am not supposed to be in here, I just couldn't stay away any longer."

"I understand, but you must go before the doctor comes in."

I hurriedly pick up my bag and find a restroom. After using the toilet, I wash my hands and splash some cold water on my face. I leave to go in search of a vending machine. My stomach is protesting, and the nausea takes hold even after a few bites of a granola bar. I sip on some water and push on.

I get startled when I hear a man crying in the hallway as his doctor explains that his wife has passed on. He's a very old man and I'm sure she must have died of natural causes. An idea instantly sparks into my head and my feet move me instinctively to the underground floor.

A short and fat, chubby little man sits at his desk writing in a chart in the hospital morgue's office. I sit down across from him and explain rather quickly what I'm asking of him. "I need you to get me across the border and this is how you are going to do it. Change the death certificate now and arrange the transport."

I pause for a moment to see if he is going to argue. "We don't have time to file so you are going to forge the document with a recent request and change the dates."

The pudgy little fucker chuckles, "I don't think you have the cash that I need in order to do this, so run along, little girl, and find a coyote to help you."

"Don't fucking play with me," my voice drops low. I unzip my bag and pull out a roll of cash which I set in front of me, then I place the handgun next to it. "Do it now," I demand.

The asshole gets to work; this is obviously not his first time. He pulls up and modifies the documents, then makes a call to an employee to come into work to make an emergency transport. After everything is set up, the man instructs the newcomer to get me across the border and drop me off in Texas.

I silently watch as they load a stretcher and body bag into the back of the ambulance. "If you are stopped, get in the bag and zip it up, or you'll be caught for sure. I put a hook on the inside of the bag." He says all this in a monotone voice, his mind detached from the words he speaks.

"*Sí*," is all I say and move along with my driver. The fat pudgy fucker goes back to his office. "I need to use the restroom," I smile nicely at the younger man I was left with.

"Knock on the cabin when you're ready." He gets inside the ambulance and starts the engine. I grab some gloves and pull them over my hands, then take the knife from my boot and quietly walk into the room where the pudgy fuck is sitting with his back to the door, holding a cell phone. Swiftly, I sneak in there and stab the motherfucker in the jugular from behind. He crumbles forward not ever seeing or hearing me coming.

I don't know the number he was about to dial, but I assume it was to one of Matias' street men. I get on his computer and wipe his hard drive with a few clicks. I walk out and, as I go, take off my gloves. I look around one more time to make sure no one has spotted me before stuffing them into a waste container.

After exiting the building, I jump into the back of the ambulance, shutting the door behind me. I loudly bang on the cab. The vehicle starts moving and I am on my way through Mexico City. I'm no idiot though. This asshole isn't planning on taking me far. I rummage through the drawers of a built-in cabinet and find a small vile of epinephrine. I fill a syringe and carefully tuck it into my bra.

While I wait for this fucker to make his move, I pull up the laptop from my bag and insert the thumb drive. I wait for it to load, then start reading the files on it.

The disgust I feel can't be any more obvious at the actions of what my husband is involved with. He and his father have made millions off shipping children and women all over the world. Exporting them as goods to be sold.

My heart sinks and I want to kill each one of these assholes myself. But with the orders tallied up on the screen, that would be impossible.

The export of drugs is horrible enough, but the thought of the monster I loved and allowed into my body while he was willingly selling people, actual *human beings*, is horrifying to me.

My child will not do this, and there is only one way to achieve this. Kill his father along with his whole family, one by one.

I get lost in reading when I feel the tires hitting a bump on the road. I look outside through the small window on the back door and notice that we are headed toward a secluded back street. I close the laptop up and wait. The ambulance finally comes to a stop. The driver exits the vehicle and I hear his footsteps approaching the back. He opens it and steps inside.

"I need a break. You need the bathroom?" He's asking me that, like he would let me get out to use the facilities but shuts the door behind him.

"I'm good, thank you." I look at the floor and wait.

His slimy hand touches my face. "If you want to get across the border, you know what I want."

I nod my head and stand, but I still don't look at him. "Fuck, I want these tits and ass." His hands run all over my body, and I allow it for the moment.

"Lie down?" I meekly squeak, "I'll do it for you."

Quickly, he lies down on the gurney, on top of the body bag. This pig really disgusts me. I climb on top of him, straddling his hips. He's not a large man, thank God for that. We are closer in size and evenly matched.

His hands aggressively rip my shirt over my head, exposing my bra. I maneuver myself to bring my feet up to rest in between his legs. His hands claw at my partially exposed body. I reach around to what looks like me undoing my bra, but my hands grab the syringe which I hurriedly uncap. I need to make sure he is distracted though, so I continue grinding my hips down into his stiff little pecker.

He closes his eyes and moans, gripping my hips. Perfect timing. My hand lunges for his neck where I jam the needle deep and push the plunger while he screams. My toes pin his balls down and I shift up slightly to put more pressure against his throat. I hold tight through the thrashing and convulsing.

The needle hits the floor and I'm about to let go because the strain on me is almost too much. But I hold on to the bitter end even though my muscles protest and shake. Finally, he limply lies there and has stopped breathing. I hurry up and remove his pants and shirt, which are part of his uniform, then put them over my own clothes.

The driver now rides as the deceased in the back and I drive the ambulance the rest of the way over the border.

I show the guard there the nurse's ID I swiped, along with the death certificate and transportation papers. He hesitates for a moment too long, so I hand out another roll of cash. He hands me back the documents and takes the cash before waving me through. He's American and I am sure that he is also paid by the Cartel to report these things. Anyone can be bought for the right price, and I know that he'll turn around and sell his secrets to any willing buyer, but I am over the border now and the air has never been so refreshing.

You see, the Hispanic people love a good story and a villain made into a hero of sorts. This is the story of how, I, Katherine Castillo, the Black Widow and Cartel princess became a Cursed Queen with no soul.

I am the wife of a Cartel boss who got pregnant and took off with his baby, leaving behind me a trail of blood. I went into hiding never to be seen again. The only woman or man to ever survive the betrayal and lies of a Cursed King to tell the tale.

That is if you can find me before I find you.

CHAPTER 15

Tank
Las Vegas, about three years ago...

Stryker called us into emergency Church.

"Blade, we need you and the boys up in Reno. Keep an eye on the sister MC, Nevada Knights. This whole situation feels like a fucking snake in the grass and I am going to kill every fucking asshole who helped Cobra."

The room is thick with anger and loss, and nothing else needs to be said because the Prez has spoken and we know what he wants. Death.

At the break of dawn, we load our bikes and head up north with determination to never fail our Prez.

We take months traveling back and forth undetected, watching their men. Killing them off like wolves. Waiting for one man to wander away from his pack, and that's when we would strike. Killing them cold and quick, then head back to report to Stryker.

With every report, he relaxes a little more but is never satisfied until we finally confirm that the Prez of the Nevada Knights MC was helping to transport in the sex trade. And Stryker loses it.

"I will drain that motherfucker myself."

We may do dirty deeds, but women and children had and always will be off limits.

With the club's numbers severely down, their Prez knew we were coming for him; it was just a matter of time.

Stryker, Mad Max, Blade, Axl, Spider and I travel up north, together this time.

Stryker kicks down the front door of the clubhouse and walks in with his pistol aimed in front of him, not even one of their members daring to try to stop us. All of them stand there with their hands raised high, and silent.

He finds their club Prez waiting for him in their club meeting room. Stryker, a force to be reckoned with, walks over without a word and shoots both of his arms up before he's close enough to pistol whip him until he's unrecognizable. Releasing pent up frustration and anger onto his face.

The man lies there limp, and Styker pushes the gun against his skull. Then pulls the trigger and blows a bullet clean through his head.

Blade, Axl and I brought in the rest of his men to watch what happens when you pussy out. We hold them at gun point, and, one by one, Stryker shoots each of them in the head. Except for two, Bear and Skid.

"You want to die like your brothers or are you going to pledge to me?" Stryker questions them.

"Pledge," they say in unison.

"Clean this shithole up."

Stryker clenches his teeth and signals us to follow him out back. He lights up the wood leftover on the firepit and tells us everything he wants carried out.

"Blade, you are going to take over this club with your men and be the man I made. Those two fuckups in there are going to lead you to head off the snake." Stryker takes out a smoke and lights it up.

Blade takes one from him and lights up with his old man. "Whatever you need, you know me and the boys have it covered. Battle Born until we die," he vows with assurance, and the three of us stand straighter behind Blade.

Stryker's evil gleam looks over his son and each one of us with pride. "The next generation of Battle Born." He nods and a hand clamps down on Blade's shoulder. "You boys make me fucking proud. You will do what needs to be done."

Stryker and Maddox head home after a few days and send a handful of men to move up here with us. We start reorganizing the club and I help Blade go over their financials, also scouring the bars for new members.

One night, within a few months of living there, I run into two cocky fucks in a bar fight, and I instantly like them. One of them I end up calling Pawn because he beat the fuck out of a man who tried to rip him off after a deal they made. The other we named Solo. Whenever shit needed done, he was the first to volunteer and would take off alone on any run.

Blade starts talking about looking around for a place after that for his tattoo shop with Axl, and calls in to Stryker who gives a recommendation of a place next to a bar called The Black Rose. How the fuck he knew of this place, I'll never know, but the man keeps an eye on everything.

I still keep up the road trips, frequently heading down to Las Vegas to check in and hand over any collections to Stryker.

Business is fucking great, and anytime I get on the road, I feel at home.

Black Widow

For the months following, I lived on the streets of Los Angeles, breaking into vacation homes and staying for a week at a time. Until I applied for a part time job as a nanny for a very wealthy couple. Using my background as a "nurse", I was easily swept into the family life. With my growing stomach and tales of a failed marriage, they took me in as their own and protected me. They helped a poor woman who was too terrified to stay alone because of an abusive ex-husband.

Through them, I met her sweet missionary sister who was unable to have children, and she became my midwife. The Hoffmans were very understanding when I left them to give birth and start over. Over the next few months, they helped me enough to hide and save some money.

What was left of my heart bled out completely when I left my son with Jane and her husband, Rick, about six months later. I kissed his soft head and inhaled his sweet scent before whispering, "Sometime in your life, I wish to hold you again, my sweet boy. I love you. Eli."

My body shook as I handed him over to Jane and walked out the door before I took him and ran. That would've been suicide because I knew that if I was selfish enough to keep him, I would be signing his death warrant. Jane agreed to keep him for me while I got my shit together.

Honestly, I have no idea if I will make it back to him in time before he is grown up. I have no other choice but to trust her with my son. But I will always be watching. I have hidden cameras all over their home and bugged everything I could think of before I left.

Living with Matias, I learned a lot about the stock market and offshore accounts and helped him to manage several of our own. I know just the right amount to gain to stay undetected. The sweet missionary lady doesn't realize I have stolen her identity online and have made her a very rich woman. One day I plan on paying her after I get my son back.

If not, and I fail, she'll have enough money to take care of him. And, hopefully, Matias never finds him.

I fall back into the darkness; in the shadows, I go to work. Embracing the skills I had been taught my whole life. A killer, con artist or a businesswoman. If it's shady, I've done it.

I start out small and find little assassin jobs while I learn the network in America and make a few allies along the way. My alias quickly became the Black Widow on the street and the tattoo of one on the inside of my wrist became my mark of a killer. Those in the trade, easily link the assassins to informants by their ink.

I've grown accustomed to the lonely life. I watch my son, Eli, from a screen every day when I can. He is on my mind both day and night. I carry him with me everywhere. I promised him I wouldn't cry, and I won't. But I turn into stone and take my pain out on the men and women that deserve to die. My agony is released with every kill, it becomes my obsession.

Right now, I watch a woman cross the street to a shithole of a crack house. Her boyfriend has been looking for her for over two years. His assumption was correct. The mother of his child began whoring out his twelve-year-old daughter for drugs.

Keeping my head down, I round the corner to the back and slip in through the unlocked door. I keep my back to the wall and creep around to where I find a middle aged, pudgy fuck molesting her daughter. He rubs her leg and promises to be gentle. The mother huffs in annoyance and puffs on her cigarette before shutting the door to the room and settling herself onto the couch where she turns the T.V. up.

Slowly, I pace my steps around the filth littered on the floor and the baby's toys. Coming up behind the worthless woman, I pull the cord out from my pocket. I wrap it tightly around my black leather covered hands.

Quickly, I swing the cord up and over her head from behind, then pull back as hard as I can with all my weight into it. My knees dig into the couch and she bucks and chokes on her sobs of desperation that make me just want her dead even faster. Eventually, she slouches and relaxes into her fate.

I run over to the bedroom door and pocket the cord to pull out a handgun with a silencer. My hand quietly twists the door open enough to get the barrel through the crack and take aim. Bam. The gun goes off and I hit that pig in the back of the head. The young girl screams, and I take off out the back before she can see me. I go around the corner and take off in a sprint down the street.

Once I reach my car, I breathe and relax. Another job done and another job closer to the man I really want dead.

Matias.

PART TWO

"I'm going to love you softly and fiercely until the day you die, I promise you this." Tank

CHAPTER 16

Black Widow
Las Vegas

The shot of tequila that's sitting in front of me is taunting me to drink it and consume the poison that's been a part of me for years already. The bartender throws me a smile from the other side of the bar. He doesn't know that I left my husband behind a year ago. I pick up the glass and hold it to my lips.

I contemplate for a second if I can take this man for a wild ride full of passion for the rest of the night before I crawl back into the shadows. My cat eyes travel over his body from head to toe. He has a nice build and a pretty face.

Tossing back the shot, I find him watching me intently for a sign to invite him into my bed and my body. My tongue snakes out to lick up the liquid drop that's rolling down from my top lip. He places two hands on the bar in front of him, and his eyes are mesmerized and caught in my web of seduction. His arms flex as he's about to say something when, suddenly, another man slides into the stool next to mine.

I raise a brow and turn my head to the right. A brazen man who looks like a Viking and wearing an MC cut smiles like the devil back at me. His dark blond hair shines from the light overhead. My fingers itch to run through his short beard. I don't smile back. I don't smile, ever. His eyes caress over my tattoos that peak out from my tank top, and over my long, black hair.

"You find what you're looking for tonight?" the Viking lays a strong arm on the bar and leans into my body, eyeing me with a knowing look. "This cat and mouse game you're playing with that dumbass is too easy. Tell me, kitty cat, are you excited?" His deep baritone washes over my body in waves.

Closing my eyes, I let his deep voice penetrate me. I involuntarily moan at the feeling of it wrapping around me tightly. My eyes snap back open to his dark blue ones.

Yes.

Our eyes agree without words, an unspoken promise to have each other for the night. I pull out a hundred-dollar bill from my bra and toss it on the bar top toward the bartender.

He was still watching, and I can feel his disappointment permeate the air from where I'm sitting. But this Viking of a man will give me what I need, I can feel it.

"Keep'em coming," I dismiss the bartender, demanding our drinks and the Viking's place in my bed.

The sound of money being whisked away, followed by a shot glass placed next to mine, and then liquid filling both of them is all just white noise. The Viking has my full attention. Our intense stare holds us captive to the other this time. This man keeps my desires peaked and ignited.

He begins to speak, but I stop him and hold my finger up to his plump lips.

"No names."

Grabbing my hand, he turns it over in his and places a kiss on the top before setting it on his leg. He points to his patch on his cut that says 'Tank'. Hard to miss.

Tank leans into my body again, "I don't need your name, but you need to know mine when you scream it later. I want to hear it cry out from this beautiful creature." Boldly, he places a chaste kiss on my lips.

My breath picks up and, like old habits, I tap it down, not wanting to give him too much. He takes my hand that is not resting on his leg and pulls it up to him. His mouth comes down and licks the flesh on my wrist with his tongue, then his teeth scrape my skin. Goose bumps cover me as he begins to sprinkle salt over the area, followed by dark and dirty ideas that begin to sprinkle into my fantasies. He devours my skin that's coated with the salt, and then kisses my lips. The intensity assaults my taste buds along with his unique flavor when his tongue captures mine.

He pulls away and sits back on his stool, then hands me my shot and we clink our glasses together before saying, "Cheers" from him and "*Salud*" coming from me. Together, we toss back the fiery liquid. Our eyes catch, watching the other as we set the glasses back down.

My eyes squint from the burn while his smile back at me. Tank's large hands delicately come up to hold my face, and I almost flinch from it. He does catch the slight shift in my body and tries to cover his reaction to me. Games. A life full of games. I will never escape.

"Make me forget, Tank," I whisper. "Make me scream your name from pleasure, and maybe just a little pain."

He holds my face inches from his, looking into my eyes for the truth in my statement. He must see my will and desire to get lost into him. He sucks my bottom lip into his mouth. Salaciously, he consumes me in this public busy casino bar in downtown Las Vegas.

This Viking and I drink into the night with only minimal words spoken. We tease each other with our promises of fulfilled desires only.

The haze cloaks around us. I can't say what made me trust this stranger, but I do trust him. I will allow him to take my body, but not my heart. He makes good on his promise and makes me scream for him multiple times into a dark hotel room.

My mind is free for this one night, but not my life.

CHAPTER 17

Black Widow

Months, maybe even a year by now, have passed since I left Tank alone and naked in the hotel room in Las Vegas. I happened to be there on a work assignment for the night and drove back to California the next morning.

Best night of my life.

The loneliness crept in and he helped me feel cherished even for a short time. But I forbid myself from hooking up again until all this is behind me.

I stare at the computer screen, not sure if I want to open the email that was sent to me. The man on the other end has an alias, Spider, within the dark web. I also know of another Spider that works with the Battle Born MC. Could this be the same Spider? My fingers tap as I mull over my choices.

It has been a few years since I fled Mexico. I've been making money by being a hit for hire, or a *Sicaria*, alias Black Widow. I have other reasons for choosing to do this, one big benefit being that it has paid my bills well. I've been comfortable, and I have been able to keep myself hidden.

The Battle Born MC has been on my radar for a long time now. I've been watching them from afar. Honestly, it doesn't surprise me a bit that they've finally reached out. I thought it would have been a little sooner since my husband was the one who had created a war for them.

From what I've dug up, they believed that my father, Cobra, was responsible for it all. In many ways, he was and he also wasn't. From what Cobra did to Fuego and Cuervo, it's been a long time coming between my old man and the Battle Born brothers by blood.

It really hurt and enraged me to find out that not only had my father had my aunt killed, but that he also had my mother murdered, like cattle. He was done with them and disposed of them like trash. He had been pissed at my mother for trying to take my sister and me away from him. Despite what my sister thought and was probably told by our father.

He was revengeful when my aunt got pregnant by Cuervo. His sister had been promised to marry a Cartel man, under the boss. He felt that he had been betrayed by both Cuervo, who was working for him at the time, mulling drugs, and by my aunt. He found revenge in killing her years later. After she gave birth to three kids, he had his men rape her and slit her throat right in front of them. Jenn, being the eldest of the kids, survived with the horrific memories.

I have plans for Cobra, for all of them who did me wrong. But my father will die first, and I am going to need help. Who takes on an MC alone, let alone the Cartel? Not a damn sane person, even with the backing of an army. It's crazy as hell, but I have no other options. I'm taking down a piece or a person at a time until I get what I want, freedom for me and my family from the Cartel.

I don't believe Battle Born knows who I am, or at least most of them don't. Cuervo and Fuego will know who I am only when they hear my name. I haven't seen them since I was a child.

I tap my finger on the laptop and think on whether I'm prepared to move forward. Eventually, I will be exposed if I go through with this. Every deal made affects the future and the battle I'm up against. Like I said, I have no other options, and my blood family means shit to me. Battle Born is the best shot I got, and we have a common enemy.

I click on the email and read the script.

Black Widow,
RE: Job for Hire
Payment depending on experience and results. Please respond to apply, interview required for position.
-Spider

Before responding, I do a quick check and reach out to some resources on the dark web to see if I can get a feel for what this could be. I set the word out to a few contacts and log off. I have another job to finish before I can even consider taking this one.

With my briefcase in hand, I head to work and drive through the heavy traffic. The California evening is stagnant with the smog and heat in the late summer air. I maneuver the car down the busy crammed freeways until I reach the hotel. I park it, never using the valet service, then strut into the bar in my blood red dress. It gives me an electric energy that's aimed toward the man I'm hunting tonight.

I order a dainty drink with an umbrella in it. Right about six o'clock on the nose, the businessman I'm waiting for walks in wearing an impressive black designer suit with a crisp white shirt. He's a damn fine looking man. Too bad he's a complete piece of shit.

I stir the sugary drink with the straw and look down at the counter. Like a magnet drawn to the bright red of my dress, he walks over and sits right next to me even though there are plenty of empty stools on either side.

After watching him for weeks, I know that he, one, always sits here, two, always goes for the girl in the bright colored, flashy dress who sits alone. Three, he rapes her after he gives her plenty of alcohol and drugs. And then, as a final insult, he always has witnesses to testify that she was more than willing to drink and then leave with him.

My client is a high paid businesswoman who was raped by this bastard. After a trial over a year ago, during which she had no proof, he was let go with zero charges. Laws are bullshit, and she found me to take out this slimy fuck.

"Evening, gorgeous, are you waiting for anyone?" His deep baritone sends chills up my spine.

I raise my head shyly, and, with a little accented twist, I say, "No, I don't have a boyfriend anymore." As I push out a pouty bottom lip, he can't take his eyes off my plump, red lips.

We spend the next fifteen minutes chatting and flirting. I move to get up before he can ask me for a refill. He may feel in control but he's being directed along by my little show.

"Good night, Mr...?" I raise a brow, and he stands to take my hand, raising it to his mouth.

"Jameson." He places a soft kiss on the top. My eyes find his, and I stare intently, drawing him in.

"You want to come up to my room?" I whisper sweetly.

He tugs me forward gently and wraps his paws around my body. We take an elevator up to a room that I already paid for with his card.

"More than anything." His hot breath heats my skin, and I suppress the gag that wants to come up. I step out of his hold just enough to turn around. He keeps a tight grip on my hip and his fingers squeeze into my flesh all the way to the room.

Once we get there, I take the key card out of my clutch and hand it over to him. I want him to walk in first.

"Sit down, Mr. Jameson, I'll get you a drink," I say with all the honey I can find to make it sweet and sultry.

He sits by the window, and I watch him while he undresses me with his eyes. The glass already has clear poison laced in, sitting at the bottom, that will stop his heart about ten minutes after ingesting it. I saunter over to him and pass him what looks like a whiskey neat.

The predator in his gaze is alarming, and, if I let him close to me, I will have about two minutes before his hands will close around my throat.

"I'll be right back, ladies' room," I explain and step back from his presence to burn some time. After about two minutes, I flush the toilet and wash my hands.

I walk out to see a very annoyed asshole by the look in his eyes. He must have not appreciated me stalling.

"Sit back, honey, I want to reward you for your patience." I tap my phone to find a slow song, then start swinging my hips back and forth. My hands run over my body and grip my tits before they are running through my hair. Slowly, before the song is about to end, I start pulling the dress up and over my head.

And then, it finally happens. I watch as he clutches at his throat and starts gasping, grabbing at his chest and pulling on his tie. "Call 911," he begs of me.

Dropping the dress that's scrunched up in my hands, I watch the lousy dick squirm before he manages to locate his cell phone. Quickly, I step forward to snatch it away from him and toss it onto the bed.

He falls forward onto his knees, reaching for me, then looks with desperation in the direction of the phone. Not too much longer and he is twitching, dying on the floor. Pretty merciful death if you ask me.

Bending over, I wrap my fingers around his wrist and check his pulse, making sure that the deadly cocktail has stopped his heart and that he's actually dead before I leave. A minute passes before his pulse is undetectable.

I stand up to put my dress back on, then start wiping the room down, removing all of my fingerprints. The glass he drank from, I pick it up from the floor and wash out the remains in the sink, then place it back on the dresser, holding it with a paper towel.

Before leaving, I grab my clutch and slip out through the joined door that connects this room to the one next door. I deadbolt it from the other side and walk into the bathroom. I take a shower and proceed to remove all the makeup I used to cover my tattoos and face, and the slutty dress, changing into a black business suit and snow-white shirt, and I snicker at that. I slip on the kitten heels I packed in the briefcase and a flowery scarf.

On a mission to get out of here as soon as possible, I wrap my hair into a tight bun pinned at the back of my head. I stuff the slutty dress and high heels into a plastic bag and then into the briefcase, then take out the burner cell and text my client an update.

Black Widow: Job done.

I wipe the phone clean of any information and then power it off, knowing that triple digits will be deposited into an offshore account into a name that no one would tie to me, Eli Lucas Taylor. My ex client and I will never talk to the other again or she will have to die to keep my secrets. I also wipe down the room I paid for of any fingerprints and leave the hotel.

A few blocks away from the building, I go inside a restaurant and sit down to have dinner alone, then go to dump the clothes in the trashcan inside their restroom. This place prides itself on cleaning the bathrooms hourly, and I'm counting on it. One less piece of shit that does not walk this earth has been taken care of.

It is a great day, so, on my way home, I grab dessert and toss my burner phone into a dumpster.

CHAPTER 18

Spider
Reno, Nevada

The Prez, Blade, along with the rest of us, have been feeling the heat to resolve our problems since we've been up here this last year or so. I went to our Prez with a wild idea to contact the Black Widow. I monitor the dark web frequently, and she has started to come in as a big player. Blade agreed, but that doesn't mean he or I liked calling in an unknown for help. We've been running out of leads and ideas and this is a Hail Mary.

About two days after sending the email to the Black Widow, I finally get a response. I was concerned that I wouldn't hear anything back from her. Between what I know from the dark places of the web and what I was able to dig up off the street, the Black Widow can help us get ahead of this mess by getting us some intel without it looking like us asking for it.

Spider,
Please call to make arrangements for a phone interview.
475-771-3695
BW

Taking out my cell, I give Blade a call and inform him that the Black Widow is ready for a conference call. Within the hour, he is ready.

Blade and his Ol' Lady, Vegas, have been hiding up in Tahoe, away from that dick, Johnny. We have been working on taking him out. So far, we know he's been helping with the shipments through our territory. We just need to find out who he's working for. Hence, the reason why we decided to call in the Black Widow.

I walk into my office to grab a new burner phone, making the call to Blade, then connect us to the number she sent me. After a few rings, she picks up and curtly speaks, "Hello. You have three minutes."

I smirk because I did trace my call to her. "We want information on the *Los Malditos Reyes* MC. I believe we have a mutual interest in taking them out. We can work together. Be at the Downtown Warehouse we own in twenty-four hours. I'll text you the address."

She doesn't confirm or say another word, just hangs up.

"Do you think she knows I was listening? How does she know who she's meeting?" Blade asks, suspicion of the woman lacing his voice, as it should.

"We've been keeping an eye on each other, and, from what I can tell, she could have intel on the Cartel and the MC down in Mexico. She's been under the radar for the most part. She is very picky about the jobs she takes. Money is not an issue. I believe it's more of an agenda that she has."

Blade lets out a long sigh. "We have to do something. Stryker is going to kick my ass when he finds out we've been hunting her since we got up here."

"We got your back, Blade, what other choice did we have? Either she's useful or we take a piece of the puzzle out of this fucking nightmare we have to clean up from the past."

I just hope like hell no one dies because of what Blade and I chose to do by bringing her in.

Black Widow

I rev the engine of my used Honda Civic that is parked outside of this dive motel on Fourth Street in Reno,

Nevada, and leave for the location Spider texted me moments ago.

Spider: 264 Keystone at 1:00 p.m.

I'm a day early, but I'm going to check out the building. Then, I'm heading to the clubhouse to stake out their MC before I decide if I'm showing up tomorrow or not.

The building on Keystone is completely empty, dark and unused, with some trash and weeds floating around. They must use this site only for very few meetings, which is both good and bad. I won't walk into their clubhouse full of bikers. They could be setting me up here too, but, if I had to choose, it would be here.

I sit for hours in my car that's parked down the street, waiting for the sun to set to see if anything, or any*one*, comes out of it in the dark. The sun has been down for hours now and nothing has moved. The building appears to be completely abandoned.

I get out of the car and take a walk to pass the building. I notice the keypad at the main entry and cameras on the outside of the building. I keep walking and looking down until I get around the corner, then go around the block.

Once I am back in my car, I grab some food and head over to the clubhouse. I park up the street at an angle so that I can use my night vision binoculars. The place is in full on party mode for the evening, at least that's what I think from the limited view I have and the amount of noise coming from inside the building.

I stick around and watch until they are worn out for the most part, then head back to the motel. Once I am there, I open the thumb drive I hid inside a lipstick case and look through the files I have gathered over the years. I don't have any updated photos of the Battle Born members up here in Reno, and that will be my next task, getting to know each one of them.

Tank pops into my thoughts while I check the locks and peek out the window before lying down for the night. Internally, I scold myself, because this is ridiculous. What am I, fifteen again?

All night, I toss and turn with dreams of killing Cobra and then Matias, the boss of the Cartel, but not getting to finish the job. What could that possibly mean?

Frustrated with myself, I get out of bed early and keep searching the web for photos to ID the MC members.

Lost in my task of scanning through the photos, I gasp when I see a photo of Tank. Shit, I knew he was a patched MC member, but I never did verify what MC he belonged too. There are hundreds of them. I was lazy that night, and now it seems I'm going to pay for it.

I suddenly remember that I have somewhere to be, and an idea comes to me. About an hour before the meet, I text Spider.

Black Widow: Location change, meet me alone on the bridge at   Idlewild Park in thirty minutes. If you're late, I'm gone.

I turn off my phone not needing a reply. He either shows up or he doesn't. I head to the park and walk around until I find a good spot to watch for him to show up.

He pulls up on his bike and parks close to where I am sitting. I don't turn to look directly at him, but his instincts kick in and he starts walking over, sitting next to me on the bench.

"Spider," he nods to introduce himself. His eyes scan over my face and tattoos, I'm sure to catalogue later. He won't be able to connect my past to the tattoos.

"We need someone to discreetly get information on the issues we are having within the club. No hit for hire, yet."

"What information are you looking for, Spider?" I turn my head slightly and look at the devilishly handsome man next to me. He has that dark hair, skin complexion and total badass bad boy look. If he were in a suit, he could easily be a Cartel Boss or a business executive. All of Matias' men look like business men and not the street thugs or gang members that they are. They have to always be able to blend in, so Spider's tattoo of a black spider on his neck would be forbidden. His tattoo only makes me wonder what kind of poison he is hiding from while warning others off.

"Mexican MC, the *Los Reyes Malditos*, is run by a man named Cobra. We have a feeling he's been setting up again to take us out, he tried years ago. We need to know what he's done and what he's doing."

At least they are looking in the right direction. I could answer all their questions right now, but this is a battle I need their help with. "If I give you the information, I want him taken out within the next few months. Those are my terms."

"I can't guarantee you that."

"I can, after the information I will give you. Let me know when you're ready." I stand up from the bench and look down at his face. "Your brothers don't need to know who I am, just tell them that I am a nurse if they happen to see me." Which will hopefully help to keep me hidden from a certain member.

Spider snorts, "I doubt you are a nurse, or that they would believe it."

"Maybe not, but I know enough to be one, and if I need to get close to anyone, it will explain my sudden presence. I'll call when I'm ready, only contact me as needed."

I turn around and start my long walk back to the car, not looking behind me. I am not worried.

He needs me alive and a secret for now.

CHAPTER 19

Tank

Sometimes I really think life plays tricks on you because, lately, I can't seem to get Kat out of my head, and my skin prickles at the thought of her.

The night at the bar in Las Vegas, as soon as I walked in, it was like my body had a radar just for her. I have the exact same feeling now that I did then. Sure, I've thought about her these last few years. I even went back to that bar a few times and asked the bartender to call me if she showed up ever again.

She never did, and the bartender is a thousand bucks richer with all the tips I left for him. I would go back and do that night over again a thousand times if I could. No bitches have compared, and shit has been boring as fuck around here with these club girls.

I want that badass bitch on my dick every night and maybe even on the back of my bike. That's a scary thought because I haven't wanted another woman on my bike since Ava, and, usually, the idea pisses me of.

I could have sworn she was around last night. I didn't even fuck the pussy that was all but laid out for me because of it. On top of that, I was in California, which makes no goddamn sense at all. It was creepy as fuck. The bitch is nearby, and I can feel it. For the last few days, I have been to every bar, looking for her up and down these roads.

Nothing.

It feels as if I'm chasing her ghost from California and back to Nevada.

I walk over to the garage where the prospects, Solo and Pawn, are working along with Axl on a few bikes.

"What's up, bro, you look a little lost. Even though you just got back from your run. We have that meet up with Skid in a few hours, yeah?"

"Aye, Skid has that meet up where we're tailing him too in a few hours."

I was sent on a road trip with the sole purpose of watching Skid, to keep him quiet and on the road, while Blade got shit set up here.

It's been a few long fucking weeks. Finally, this shit is going to end tonight. We got the information we needed, and we are taking this traitorous asshole down.

"Nah, the Road Dog is never lost." I stop to think and place one hand under my chin and rest my elbow on my opposite arm. "But he is looking for something," I absently say looking around with a huff.

"Okay, what are you looking for then?" Axl stops working and stares at me, a bit lost with my theatrics.

Dragging the stool over, I take a seat next to where they're working. "You remember the club war a few years back? Right about a year after that, I ran into this bitch at the bar after a road trip down there. You went to bed early."

Axl slowly nods along, "Yeah, I think so. Why, are you dating her, or ran into her again? Dude, did she show up with a *baby*?!" His eyes flare just a little, dramatic bastard.

My head whips back surprised at the thought, "Fuck no! I hope that shit never happens to me. I just feel like she's around, and I got that shit on my mind, is all."

"Oh, I see, you can't get that snatch off your mind, you need another round. Call her up and take care of that then." Axl tosses the rag at me while he starts picking up the tools around his bike.

"I don't have a clue where to even find her."

Axl stands up straight and his eyebrows almost touch. "What is her name? Have Spider help you hunt her down."

I take a deep breath because I'm really fucked. "Well, I don't know that either. You see, she didn't want to exchange names, and I just called her Kat."

"Hot. Still, go talk to Spider. You may be surprised at what he can find out."

I toss the rag back at his chest and take a few steps towards the door before I hear another set of footsteps behind me. I turn around and raise my eyebrows at Axl.

"What? I need to find out what happens, let's go," Axl chuckles with his hands out, and then shoulder checks me to get my feet moving again.

Shaking my head at the nosy fucker, I let him follow me to the security room where we bump into Spider who's walking in himself.

The grumpy bastard doesn't say anything at first, taking a seat in front of his computers, then turning around to face us. "What are you two fuckheads up to and why are you in here?"

"I'm good, thanks for asking, Spider. I need to find someone."

"Like who? I have shit to do," he snaps at us, and Axl proceeds to fill him in for me like a little snitch bitch.

"He has a girlfriend he needs to bag and doesn't know shit about her. I need you to find her for him so I can see if this actually happened, or he's just trying to compete with me again since Dana came into the picture." Dana is the best friend of Vegas, Blade's Ol' Lady. He's been desperately trying to hook up with her after multiple failed attempts so far.

I turn to look at Axl, exasperated with his big ass ego, and he turns to me satisfied with his recount of the situation. "What the fuck are you talking about?" I whisper yell my disbelief to his smug face. "You have not fucked that woman, no fucking way." I slash my hand through the air to help my case.

"I didn't say I did, not that I would tell you because it's all MY cherry pie, and I wouldn't share with you dirty fucks. I said- you need a girlfriend because I am lining mine up. She knows it, I know it, and you do too. Like I said, you need to keep up with me." Axl thumps his chest to make a point.

"Get the fuck out!" Spider growls at us in a warning tone that tells us that he's not going to put up with us.

Both of us turn at the same time from our stand off. "Sorry, Spider, that was rude. Can you please help?"

"Tell me about it," he grinds out.

I start explaining my night with Kat in detail. The whole time, he sits there like a judge, with a scowl on his serious face, soaking in the information, to prove what, I don't know, until he says slowly, "Did you ever think that maybe she doesn't want you to find her? She straight off said, do not give me your name and I'm not giving you mine. She takes all evidence of your gag worthy night, of which I didn't need the screaming and back scratching details—"

My lip quirks up in half a smirk, and I interrupt him, "That was a bonus, just for you." I shrug off the irritation from him.

He proceeds on ignoring me. "She ghosted you for a reason, Tank. She wanted a lay with no attachments. How am I supposed to find her off a description of her Latina heritage, cat eyes and banging ass? The tattoos, maybe. I'm not a private investigator."

He ends his long rant glaring at me, lost in thought for a moment. His eyes open slightly and then he holds back whatever crossed his mind.

Interesting, he *does* know something.

It may not be as hard as I thought to find my K-Love.

CHAPTER 20

Black Widow

I hadn't thought too much of my night with Tank, that is until I saw his picture, then the club patch up close and personal on Spider's cut. Shit.

I can try and keep things exclusive and let Spider and Blade know that the brothers can't know who I am for the sole reason of the Cartel finding me again. The real reason being, I can't run into Tank again.

The *one* time I itched so bad to have the feel of a man's hands on me again, and I really fucked it up. Once they figure out who I am and they share it with the rest of their club, I will be out of hiding, and it won't be long before the club and Matias, the man I ran from, come face to face and he will find me again.

I have way too much at stake here, too much to lose. I purposely pushed Tank away from my thoughts for that very reason, and took off like a bat out of hell. He is going to be pissed if he finds me. He, along with his brothers, will want to know why I fucked him that night. And it does look like I targeted Tank, except that

I didn't. I was targeting any dick to give me a banging orgasm for the night and scratch my itch.

Tank zeroed in on me as soon as he walked in that bar and volunteered his fine ass up for the job. I knew I should have said *no* and knew better than to tangle him up in my web, but I was selfish, and I wanted him. I craved him to dominate me and make me forget.

The dangerous combination of these and of who he actually is, may send me back deep into the shadows, to hide. For his sake and my own. Fucking me again would kill him.

Goose bumps start covering my skin as a flashback hits me hard. My body remembers him better than my mind. I see it all again in my head, how Tank ripped every piece of clothing off me and him as soon as we got inside the room. His hands were mesmerizing, and so was his tongue as it went over every part of my flesh. There was not a part of our bodies left undiscovered before he lifted my legs up and around his massive body and fucked me hard against the foyer wall.

He was so forceful but thoughtful, like he could read my mind. My body shivers at the thought of the connection I experienced with him. Now I wonder how I will survive this because of that one selfish night.

I hadn't been with a man since Matias and then there was Tank. The contrast between the two men confused me. Did Matias teach me to crave the pain and intensity? But, with Tank, he was those things but also something so different that I couldn't understand it.

All this worry may be for nothing, he could be down in the Las Vegas chapter. Except, I'm no fool, and I know it will all catch up with me, eventually. Best I can do is to get to know the club routine and work around his schedule, maybe create a little diversion if I need to, and send him on a road trip.

I smirk to myself as I picture sending him, the Road Captain, on a wild goose chase. I laugh at the thought, and it stuns me. I haven't laughed in years. It shocks the shit out of me, and I stop immediately. Why do I find this so funny? Just what the hell am I doing here?

Shaking off the ideas, I mellow out and get back to my game plan of making a checklist of what needs to be done. First, I know that Alessia DeRosa, also known as Vegas, and Jenn are my cousins. Vegas and Jenn work together along with Dana and the three of them have been best friends since birth. Jenn is also Cuervo's daughter.

I remember very little of Jenn's mother from when I was little. There was a blonde girl I used to play with, but the memory is fuzzy. I'm curious if seeing Jenn again will help me to remember if it was possibly her or not.

What if *she* remembers *me*? It could happen, but from what I would guess from her past, she won't remember much at all. Our mothers were always meeting in secret. My father wouldn't allow her to visit family. As a child, I didn't know that I had an aunt from my father's side. It makes more sense now why my mother never told me who they were and called them her friends.

These secrets are going to blow up in all their faces. I feel bad about how that will affect these girls, but they aren't my secrets, and it's better to face them before my father, Cobra, the MC Prez in Mexico, or the Cartel do much more to them than they already have.

Second, I need to find out exactly what the MC wants and give them only the information they need while I see if my plan works. That is what I am going to tell Blade and Spider, that my identity is for me to know alone, until they can be trusted. I will only meet with Spider until further notice, one contact, that's it.

I can't be seen in public or spotted, but I do need to know these faces and to be able to spot them all at a glance. First stop is to Johnny Carmine's office and check on what this dirty fucker is up to.

I park my car down the street and get out. I walk into a little restaurant and order some food while watching the building across from me. I sit by the window and read a women's magazine with page after page of recipes.

My hamburger arrives just as I spot Johnny walking into the building along with another man, and I zero in on the latter. He's definitely sexy and dangerous looking, and he probably deals with Johnny under the table, off the books. I write his license plate down as I scarf down my burger. I throw a tip on the table and go out to my car to sit and wait for my dark and dangerous, albeit unknown, target to walk out.

Eventually, he is back in his car. We merge into traffic, and I hang back far enough to allow him plenty of space. He finally slows down and comes to a stop in a parking lot behind a downtown casino. I park around the front, then rush to see if I can follow him through the same door he just walked through.

I see a guard at that entrance door and decide that I need to get inside the casino's floor, go and shake some businessmen's hands just so that I can get into that private party. I hurriedly race back to the motel I've been staying in, dress in a black cocktail dress, and hightail my ass back to the casino.

I walk around the floor after I pay for my own stack of chips and start observing the tables. I pick one man in an expensive suit and being too flashy with his stack of cash, and saddle up to that table to place a bet there. He'll be easier to bait since his ego will be bigger than his sense. Within moments, he's putty in my hands and has me blowing on his dice for good luck.

"Where are you from?"

"Florida, baby. It's my last night here and I'm looking for a good time, you up for that?" He rolls the dice and scores a small payoff.

I play along and the action gets really fun when I suggest, "You know where the real fun is in this place?"

His face lights up wanting to impress me, and he takes me downstairs to where the real bets are. I stick close by his side like the good little arm candy I am supposed to be, and take the room in.

High-end bets are being placed on the cage match, and, not to mention, the high-end call girls on the men's arms, which is exactly what I look like.

While the suit makes his bet on the next fight, he talks to me and I flirt along while he paws at my body. We walk closer to the cage and I watch the room, pretending to cheer on the fight until I finally find my target from earlier, the guy who met up with Johnny.

"Who is that guy?" I ask the suit, nodding across the room. "He looks like the manager here?"

The suit looks put off, like I'm about to go jump the guy's dick right in front of him. "Yeah, he's Tony Riva," his hand touches my cheek, "I wouldn't fuck him though if I were you, you're too sweet for that kind of action."

I roll my eyes at him like a schoolgirl and swat at his chest. "I wouldn't, I'm having a great time with you, sexy."

He wraps his large hand around my ass and grinds his hardening dick into my stomach. So badly I want to throat punch this fucker for treating me like a piece of meat. I continue to play it cool until he suggests, "It's getting late, you ready to take this upstairs?"

I push the fake giggle out and nod yes. "Let me run to the restroom first?"

We all know that as soon as I got out of his hold and sight, I'm gonna be long gone.

See ya, Florida man.

CHAPTER 21

Tank

I never in my wildest dreams thought I would see her again.

Kat.

I think she could be my wife, though it's really hard to remember that night clearly with the amount of tequila we drank.

Usually, the bitches hang around for my morning wood. Not this one though. She was gone like a figment of my imagination. I had to check the floor for the condom I tossed, and it wasn't even there. It was like I just said, never fucking happened. But here she stands with even more ink since the last time I saw her a couple of years ago.

"I can't believe she's real," Solo, the little dick, snickers. "Axl kept on saying earlier that you had a fake girlfriend to help with your self-confidence." He shrugs after that.

My fist flies to my right, nailing the little fucker in the shoulder, and he falls into Pawn, the other little shit prospect I sponsored into this club. I'm so moonstruck at the sight before my eyes that I can't beat these two up properly.

Axl told me to pick up the "nurse" for her to look over the kids at the warehouse. The woman standing outside of the beat up Honda in that skin tight black dress is no fucking *nurse.*

What the fuck is she doing, I'll find out soon enough. Right now, we have club business to get to, and, somehow, these fuckers know her. I plow forward like a bull, ready to reunite with her. My body towers and then covers hers when she steps back against the wall.

"I caught you again, Kitty Kat."

I rest my body forward on one hand against the wall while a finger from my other hand runs up the outside of her thigh, to her hip, then waist where I stop and lightly squeeze before whispering, "You've been summoned by Blade to check on the merchandise we commandeered, and he wants a nurse to look the kids over." I kiss the side of her cheek. "Get dressed for it, K–Love."

She pants out a few deep breathes before her shell shocked and excited face, because, let's face it, it's me, snaps out of it, and she stands up tall and strong, gritting out, "Back the fuck up."

"Get moving, Kat," I order, but, at the end, I struggle to keep the laughter from spilling out.

"No."

"Yes."

She glares at me, then, ever so slightly, looks at what I'm sure are the surprised faces of Pawn and Solo.

"Move, or I'll take you like this, I don't give a fuck."

I push off the wall, giving her enough space to get into her room. Before she can shut the door in my face, my boot stops it from closing. "Keep it open and dress out here, you are not slipping out on me again."

Kat's eyes squint and her mouth quirks up. Before I know what's happening, she starts pulling on the bottom of the dress, slowly dragging it up and over her head. Fuck me, she's covered in tattoos which barely show any bare skin on her body.

"What's going on?" Solo asks from behind me, and I can hear and feel him at my side. I take my hand that was holding me up off the door frame and catch his face from getting any closer, pushing him back. No way in fuck is he seeing this. She's mine.

He stumbles back and curses, but I'm lost in the moment as I'm staring intently at the red bra and thong that's in contrast with her dark skin. Blood starts pumping through my body and my hands ache from not being able to touch her.

She bends over, sticking her ass up high, and her long black hair cascades down to the floor. She keeps an eye on me while she pulls a black shirt over her arms, very effectively shielding herself from me.

While I'm tracking her every move, she sits on the bed and easily slides a pair of black leather pants up her legs. She kills me when she stands to pull them up, then steps into a pair of knee-high leather boots. Fuck. Bending over again, the deviant woman slowly zips them up to her knees.

She picks a bag off the floor and saunters over to me. Careful not to touch me, she whispers, "Cat got your tongue?"

My little tease pushes my body back with one hand to my chest, and out the door she goes. I willingly allow it because, if I don't, the wood sporting a tent in my pants would fuck the hell out of her after the most erotic backward striptease I've ever witnessed.

Kat drops her hand from my body and saunters toward her car. My head catches up to what we are doing. I shut the door to the motel room, then move to stop her from getting inside. "You ride with me, Kat."

She whips around, shooting a furious glare at me. "Like fuck I'm going anywhere with you. I'll follow you in my car."

"Like fuck you are!" I bark back at her. She widens her stance and I charge forward, pick her up and throwing her over my shoulder. The goddamn woman kicks, aiming for my nuts, and I laugh before easily tossing her into the back seat of the Suburban.

"Sit next to her." Pawn and Solo jump in the back, flanking her on either side. They better watch their throats and dicks.

We ride in silence on the way to the warehouse, and every time I look into the rearview mirror, all I see is Kat. She scowls at me with heat that I'm sure is a mixture of hate and lust. I glare back because I can tell you one thing. This woman needs me to spank that ass. A lot.

Kat obviously has a lot of pride and hides herself to keep others away. Only one thing will make her show the truth, a man's loving hand. One that can break through to her hard shell, and I'm that man. I can feel her like she's a part of me, and I'm never going to let go.

I pull the Suburban into the warehouse and park. I jump out of the driver's seat, not bothering with shutting the door before ripping open the back one.

"Move," I order Pawn, and he too jumps out. My hands pick Kat up from her seat and toss her body over my shoulder again, then march into the warehouse.

"Tank! You freaking, big assed asshole! Put me down! I said I would help!" Kat bellows as I open the door and walk through with her.

I reach up and lay down a hard smack right on her leather covered ass. Kat's long black hair flies through the air as her back arches from the blow.

"Easy, Kitty Kat, you're scaring the kids, and the boys are about to shoot your loud, mouthy ass. It's a nice ass, though, and I don't want them to shoot it, K-love." I rub the spot I smacked, making her squirm more.

I pull her down the front of my body. Her tits press against my chest, and I suppress the urge to not let her go, but I do it, gently placing her on her feet.

She shoves away from me with both hands planted on my chest. Or, at least, she tries to, and I laugh a little. She glares while my body slightly shakes. I kiss the end of my fingers and tap her nose. "Calm down, Kitty Kat, we can play later," I tease and wink at her.

Grabbing her temples, she rubs circles and takes in deep breaths before dropping her hands and storming forward to stand in front of the table.

"Hey, I'm Kat, you must be the president of these merry little misfit fuckers?" She sticks her hand out to Blade.

"Blade, and yes, I'm the president," he answers with a slight change in his face, trying not to smile at her. "You a nurse?" He looks over her and continues, "Can you check these kids over? Help us find them some safe places to go?"

She gives in a little and breathes out slowly. "Yes and yes. Tank, haul in my bag, k, hot stuff?" Kat holds her hand out for the young girl in front of her, then takes her in another office to look her over.

Kat

My head feels scrambled trying to keep up with everything that just happened. Did I just introduce myself as *Kat* to their *president*? Shit. What was I supposed to do? This man is so far into my head, he's like quicksand and I'm slowly being pulled under. I didn't know what to say to their Prez.

I couldn't lie and give my fake alias name. I went on instinct and used the name that Tank gave me. Some part of me likes it. How did he ever pick a nickname so close to my own name?

Freaking Tank is my kryptonite. Had it been anyone else, I would have shot him and gotten myself out of there, but I didn't. I couldn't turn him away again. Just like at the bar, and I knew better. He disarms me, and I need to figure it out, soon.

The scared teenager sits down next to me and I ask her a few questions. Thank God she wasn't abused or harmed in any way, not physically at least. She and her friend are just naive kids that got themselves into a whole lot of trouble with very bad men. Tami could've been the one raped or sent overseas by my father and the Cartel.

"I don't know where they took Amanda," she cries and folds over into her chair, covering her face. I rub her back and silently vow to help with finding her friend. Give her the same freedom and grace Tami just got by escaping the fate she's currently in. The pain, however, none of us can escape that.

"Tami," I gently call her name. She sits up and looks up at me. "You got into some shit, but you are okay now. Don't worry, I will make sure you are okay. You can trust me."

She says okay, but her heart is not in it. I know this isn't my fault or my mess, but some fucked up piece of me wants to make this right for her. I couldn't save my sister in the end. She turned against me, but if I can save this girl, it'll be a small win to all the losses that have left a gaping hole that's been bleeding with pain.

Tank walks into the office with my bag and I grab my first aid kit. I clean up all the kids' bumps and bruises while he stands next to me, helping me by handing me items from it as needed. Solo and Pawn thoughtfully bring in sandwiches and drinks for everyone.

Together, the four of us make them beds the best that we can with the supplies they brought from the store. I walk up to Spider when I see him walk into the warehouse hours later.

"Thanks a lot, asshole," I say under my breath.

"What's the matter, *Kat*, are you hiding something? Or from someone?" He tilts his head over to the side and watches me closely. "You have a lot of fucking explaining to do, and, don't worry, I will get to the bottom of it."

"My past is my business until I decide when to bring you into it. Or are we going to war too, Spider?" I threaten back. If he thinks he can push me around, he's fucking wrong.

"What's going on here?" Tank stands firmly at my back. The feeling is a little too comforting. We need to talk. This shit is all so fucked up.

"Nothing, brother, came to check on what's going on. I'm heading back to the club." Spider's impassive face watches me, and I follow him with my eyes as he leaves us.

"Kat." My eyes close because I can't have another man like this, one that can destroy me with his promises. "Go get in the Suburban, we have men to watch over the kids until we figure out what's going on tomorrow."

My body feels exhausted and the fight is gone for the day. I give in, and, without looking, I walk out to the car and get into the front passenger seat, resigned to my fate.

I'm clearly on their radar, at least firmly on Spider's, and he will dig until possibly exposing me without even realizing what he'd done.

Signing my death warrant.

CHAPTER 22

Kat

It doesn't surprise me when we pull into the clubhouse parking lot, so I don't argue and follow Tank inside.

"Kat, have a seat at the bar, we have church or a—"

I wave him off, "Club meeting, go. I know what you're saying."

His eyes scrunch together, and I want to laugh. He'll put it all together soon enough. I find the bar area by myself, even though I can feel his eyes piercing my back. "We will talk soon enough, I'll be here," I point to a chair and sit my ass in it.

When I look back up, he has a handsome smile on his face that shatters my heart because I can very well shatter his in moments, and I'm only here because it's the best move for me right now. I would leave him at a drop of a hat to save myself, to do what I have to. This is killing me because I know that he would be worth the pain to try if I could.

While I nurse a beer as I'm waiting for him to come out, I watch the people milling around the club and get a feel of the environment. The prospect behind the bar, or anyone else that comes by, doesn't say a word, and I'm fine with that.

Until a woman's voice catches my attention. "Yo, Pawn, make me a vodka tonic?"

The brunette hands him her purse and sits down a stool away from me along with a blonde woman. Not hang arounds. Possible Ol' Ladies? The brunette instantly looks at me with interest and I'm questioning how this will go down.

She gives me a chin lift and points to herself then the blonde, "Vegas. This is Dana. You?"

"Kat," I answer quickly, not wanting to give too much away.

Pawn, the prospect, interjects the introductions, "Vegas is Blade's Ol' Lady, and Dana belongs to Axl."

"I don't belong to Axl." Dana's eyes are scrunched together, annoyed he claimed her to him.

Before I can stop myself, I ask, "Sure you want to say that out loud where these club whores and their crew can hear you?" I wait a moment to see if it pisses her off that I said anything, but it doesn't seem to, so I continue. "Way I see it, if you're not claimed, good for you, but you also invite those whores to make passes at Axl, or his brothers to do the same to you. Just saying, either way, be sure." I take a long pull from my beer and wait.

Vegas smiles, "Who's got a claim on you?"

Enjoying a normal, more genuine conversation, I keep talking, "Ah, wouldn't you like to know?" I tease.

Vegas puts her glass back onto the bar top, assessing me, coming up with, I'm sure, a few ideas of who I belong to.

Pawn jumps in and puts us out of our misery again. "Tank's lady." I glare daggers at the little shit for ruining my game. Who says I belong to Tank?

Dana laughs, "That big pain in the ass is after you, huh? No wonder you could read my face. Misery loves company. Move over here, we need to join forces against those two."

Dana seems to be more reserved so when she says, "A pitcher of lemon drop shots. Please," it's confirmed. Misery does love company.

"Shit-faced for three coming up!" Pawn says, not as excited about this as we are. He makes a pitcher of them, sliding three shot glasses our way, along with it.

Dana holds her glass up to us, "Here's to the love we thought we had, to the love we want, and to the booze to drown out the empty space in between." The three of us clink glasses and down the shots.

Dana's toast almost breaks me, and my skin begins to crawl with the pain of the past. She has no idea what she said and how much it hurts.

The love we thought we had, to the love we want.

I drown my feelings in booze until it doesn't hurt quite so much. Pawn holds out a joint for us and announces, "Straight cut, primo green, not laced, you ladies enjoy." He smiles like a proud poppa.

Taking the joint from his hand, I place it in between my lips, then lean across the bar to Pawn. He lights it and winks at me while I take a deep pull in before passing it over to Vegas.

A tiny chuckle escapes me when Dana takes the smallest, cutest drag from the joint, and Vegas smiles with pride. Aw, must be her first time. She passes it to Pawn, who drags, passes and blows.

The brothers start entering the room, and I wait in anticipation of one face, Tank's. He walks in and stops right behind Vegas and Dana. He doesn't look too pleased that I'm sitting with them. I'm too buzzed to care though.

Blade lights a fresh joint and drags from it, then hands it to Tank. Blade starts to shotgun with Vegas, at least from what I can see out of the corner of my eyes. My main focus, if you can call it that, is Tank.

I can't hear much over their lovey dovey words as I try to keep my blood at a normal rate. It's hard to do when Tank's hand sneaks under my shirt and starts tracing my skin with a finger.

Dana and Axl flirt with each other and pass along sweet words of love to the other that I try my best to tune out and ignore. Vegas, though, high as a kite, enjoys the show of affection.

"Fuck, Blade, he just killed it with that one, that even made me feel a little shaken up," she awes over her friend.

"You dickheads are really putting me in a tight spot here." Tank looks a little lost for once.

"Easy, lady killer, you don't have to confess your undying love for me. Keep it casual, big guy." Patting his chest, I try not to choke on the rush of emotion, of *love*, that's suddenly running through me.

That fucking shit will kill from the inside out, leaving you alone and empty.

CHAPTER 23

Tank

The pain that flashes across Kat's eyes stings in a way that I wasn't expecting. My hand wraps around hers, and, for the first time in my life, I want to protect someone other than my brothers.

Tugging her off the stool, I lead us down to my room. I shut the door behind us, then gently take her beautiful face in my hands, looking at the woman I dreamed about for so long. It hardly seems to be real, high or not. How is this possible?

I'm not able to stop myself from softly touching my lips to hers, to feel what I craved for so long.

"Don't be soft with me, Tank, please."

She begs for me to not be soft, why? Does she suffer from a broken heart and past? Being rough with her would only show her the animal she wants me to be. I'm not the monster in her dreams and never will be.

Ignoring her request, I do what I want anyway because who knows how long I'll have her. I'll take her however I need and be selfish with her, then figure out the rest later.

My hands begin to tenderly remove the clothes from her body, one by one. I toss her shirt away and remove her boots, which are followed by her pants and lacy red underwear.

My hands roam over her skin as I lead her over to the bed to lay her down. When I bend over, I kiss across her heart for a moment. She freezes but her breathing gives away the rawness of her feelings. With a light touch, I spread her legs wide and sit between them, resting them on either side of my body. I caress her breasts while my lips taste her salty sweet skin, down to her stomach.

"I don't understand this, Tank," she confesses quietly into the dark. "How do you do this to me?"

I don't answer, not knowing the answers myself, and follow my path down her body until I reach her pussy. My hands hold her hips and my tongue takes a sensual lick of a long lost home, my woman. Sweetly and slowly, I build her up with tender licks and sucks until she is panting desperately for more.

Pushing my tongue more firmly against her clit, she lets go of a moan that sounds like a love song to my heart. I keep the pressure until she grinds her hips even harder against my face. I give her what she wants and add two fingers into her cunt, pumping them in and out until she is screaming my name as she's squeezing my fingers.

Before she comes down all the way, I rip the shirt away from my body and pull out the condom from my wallet. I push my pants down like an eager kid and wrap up my dick like an expert. I hover over her before plunging inside her hot and ready cunt, and love the shit out of it with every thrust.

Kat wraps her legs up and around my waist. Her hands roam through my beard and her eyes memorize my body. "You're not going anywhere, Kat, you're not leaving me again." She wants to believe me, but she can't lie to me. I see the secrets swirling around in her eyes.

Her legs tighten when I pick up my pace, and my eyes close when I come from the contractions of her pussy squeezing my dick. I drop on top of her and cradle her body to mine.

My lips capture hers before I answer her question from before. "I don't understand how, but I know who you are to me, and you do the same to me. You make my heart beat alive just with your presence. That's what you do to me."

I slide out and lie down next to her. I remove the condom and toss it onto the floor, then pull her into my body, wrapping my leg and arm over her.

"Did you really just toss the condom on the floor? God, that's gross, Tank."

"I aimed for the trashcan," I laugh a little. "Go to sleep. Tomorrow I'm going to fuck you without being fucked up for once, and you are going to be here in the morning because the prospects are told not to let you leave this building. No escaping me this time, Kitty Kat."

When she doesn't answer, I repeat her words from earlier, "*Cat* got your tongue?"

She lets out a deep soulful laugh that makes me laugh with her. We fall asleep together, wrapped around each other.

As I drift off, I can't help but thinking that it will be a tough road ahead, but, eventually, we are going to be solid.

Kat

I wake up with an unfamiliar feeling of a man resting beside me. Jesus, love fucking hurts, and my heart beats hard when I open my eyes for a moment to confirm that, in fact, there *is* a man next to me.

Shit, what the hell am I doing? Goddamn it. All it does is rip your heart out and leave you feeling like your chest is on fire.

My thoughts race with the rush of possibilities of love, then fear paralyzes them, the ideas, before my heart takes off. My mind catches on and I freeze the thoughts of forever, pushing those feelings away. My heart becomes numb and stone to the world.

I crawl out as slowly as possible without waking him up, and start looking for my clothes that are scattered around the room. I put them on just as the early dawn light starts shining through the window.

Tank said the prospects would be watching for me, and that stops me from putting my boots on. He's going to know as soon as I leave.

My hands hold a boot in midair, and I look back over to him. I want to crawl back in bed with him. When I was younger, I would have.

The stubborn and wiser part of me wins over because love is a risk I can't afford to gamble with right now. With my head back on straight, I place my feelings on lockdown, my heart cold and hard as ice. I am dead set to come out the victor in this game where Tank has no idea what is going on, and he can't be a distraction. I can't lose.

I pick up the other boot and tiptoe over to the door. My hand is steady as it ever so slowly turns the knob. I jump back and let go when Tank's large one comes down onto mine.

"Kit Kat, where are you going?" His big body steps forward and pushes mine against the wall. My eyes squint at him, annoyed that he stopped me and that I was caught. "You aren't going anywhere, love." His hands incase my face and his lips crash down on mine.

He takes things from me without asking, and a part of me wants to love it, but the other part knows better. I bite his lip and tear away with my teeth, fighting him for dominance. His head jerks back and he licks where I bit him, tasting his own blood. His eyes narrow in on my own.

"Before you pick a fight, Kat, make sure you can win. Don't fucking bite me and think shit won't happen to that ass."

He rips the shoes from my hands and throws them on the floor behind him. I didn't notice before now, but the man is naked and very hard. He pulls the shirt up and off my body. Like a hurricane, he has my bra off, his hand in my hair, pushing me to the floor onto my knees before him.

He tugs my head back with a firm grip and growls down at me, "Bite me, K-Love, I fucking dare you."

Some sick part of me loves his dark and twisted side. The smirk on my lips and the smile in my eyes lightens his grip just enough to let me move.

"Hands behind your back," he grinds out, and I do as he asks, holding my hands together while my mouth sucks his dick into the back of my throat, apologizing for my behavior the only way that I can, with submission.

Tears leak down my cheeks from the forceful thrusts he delivers in and out of my mouth. He gathers more of my hair into his hand into a ponytail, gaining more grip and control of the momentum.

My teeth scrape lightly on his shaft giving him the naughty cat he loves so much. Tank becomes wild and unhinged with passion with the small twinge of pain. His eyes shine with approval at the sight of saliva that drips from my mouth.

"You my dirty girl, Kat?" He moans before ripping me away and jacking off, his dick shooting his cum over my chest. He groans at the sight of my tits covered in him.

He pulls me up and gives my mouth a tender kiss, then fucks me with his tongue next. It's his way of saying that he accepts me just the way I am. He removes my pants and lays me out on the bed, eating my pussy before breakfast.

I'm really fucked when it comes to Tank.

CHAPTER 24

Tank

It's been weeks since Kat looked at me, or even acknowledged me. Blade mentioned that she took a job working at The Black Rose. She also has been helping the kids get set up in group housing over in California, then herself and Tami into a place of their own. I know that Spider put their place under an unknown name so that it wouldn't come back to any one of us.

While she's also been busy working, Kat has found the time and creative ways to keep me at an arm's length.

Blade wanted someone with Vegas, looking after her twenty-four-seven, and I've been crashing on her couch since she took a beating inside the building of her new brewery. Since all the shit that went down with the club, bitch has proven that she is strong though, and she's been recovering well considering the fucked-up shit that went down.

The Club has taken over any plans I had of pursuing Kat further with this fucked up mess. I've kept tabs on her from a distance and I know she has on me too.

Whenever we are close by, we know the other is near. She has a lot of secrets and I plan on uncovering each one of them.

You may think I'm crazy and should find an easier woman. But she is *it*. I'm no fool either. This shit she is wrapped up in is big if my best friends and, or the Prez, and Sargent in Arms are keeping it a secret. If Blade and Spider are keeping this between them, it's some heavy shit if both Axl and I don't know, not to mention the national Prez, Stryker. There is a damn good reason for it.

Tonight, we finished the business up at the mines, with CC, that slut, buried her deep in the desert, never to be thought of again. Blade got his revenge on CC for her hand in Vegas losing their baby.

Still, we have another debt from the past to clean up. See what I was saying, we've been putting shit back together for the past few years, barely keeping up with it all. I'm gonna need some vacation time soon, this shit is soul draining.

Tony Riva, the partial casino owner, seems to think he has our nuts in a vice to pay his ass back for the past president's mistakes. He does, for now. The brothers and I are down at the casino waiting for Pawn to fight, and, if all goes as planned, Kat will be working the bar tonight for the patch-in party for the prospects.

Maybe I'll get lucky and corner her ass and get some answers or maybe more? That is a great fucking idea and I need Pawn to get his ass to work so I, I mean *we*, can get the fuck out of here.

Pawn is a scrappy little fucker. I found him and Solo getting into some stupid shit when I picked up these pound puppies. I smirk thinking of Kat and her nickname for these little fucks. I slap him hard on the back. "Don't fuck around with the dude, go in and lay him out. He plans on making it stretch out for a payoff. Go at him hard."

Pawn gives me a fist bump and tosses me his shirt before getting into the ring where he jumps back and forth, waiting for the other fighter to come in.

His opponent has a good fifty pounds on Pawn. "He's gonna get hit hard, but he can handle it," I tell Axl who gives me a doubtful look. Trust me, I know. Blade has had us watching these fighters, and this one asshole has a good left hook that will catch Pawn off guard at least once.

Finally, the diva motherfucker shows up and jumps into the ring. As predicted, he has Pawn chasing him around the ring a bit until Pawn finally has him cornered. He goes for the body and doesn't see the left hook coming.

Pawn stumbles back from the blow a bit but comes right back with a kick to his gut and then an uppercut. They go at each other, and Pawn does deliver a good show.

Tony sits over in his VIP section. I wave my fingers when he catches me looking at him. Axl elbows me.

"What, he was staring." I laugh at him because, whatever, Tony is a little bitch.

Pawn gets down and dirty taking the fighter to the floor with a leg sweep and beats his face in with his fists. The bell is rung, and, again, Battle Born takes the win. I can't stop smiling at the bloody mess Pawn made as I toss him his shirt before we haul ass to the bar for the after party.

The guys all congratulate Pawn on our way to the bikes. "Not only did you kick ass, but tonight is the first patch-in party since Blade took over as Prez. Let me make sure you all realize that *I* brought in these two to the club. You are welcome."

The brothers shake their heads, but, whether they like it or not, it's true. We jump on our bikes and eat up the pavement to the after party to patch these two fucks into the club.

Solo walks in with a limping Pawn, helping him now that the endorphins probably wore off. Collective gasps sound in the air at Pawn's swollen and bruised up face.

Axl walks in behind them, with me and Spider in tow. Axl belts out to the crowd, "You should see the other guy!" The crowd chuckles as he continues, "This pissant fucker gave it back to that asshole twice as hard." Axl slaps Pawn's back, causing him to wince in pain.

Blade stands up, directing the attention to himself. "Solo, Pawn, bring your scrawny asses over here."

As they walk toward Blade's table, which is the one closest to the bar, he continues, "You two, over the past year and some change, have proven yourselves and your dedication to the Battle Born brothers. This," Blade points around the room, "Is your patch-in party. Don't be stupid," Blade finishes and sits back down while Pawn and Solo fist bump the air with a "Fuck yeah" from both. They then turn to face each other and begin giving manly back slaps and fist bumps to one another.

All the guys cheer for the newest members when Axl hands them their new patches and rips off the Prospect ones from their cuts.

Tami comes running over with ice for Pawn and pulls up a chair for him. The brothers laugh at her worry and the care that she shows for him. Her face blanches, feeling embarrassed, and she turns around, taking long strides back behind the bar.

Kat turns from handing a beer over the counter and glares daggers at the men. Abruptly, they all get quiet.

I can't help but laugh at the scene. "My little kitten has sharp claws, don't ya, Kitty Kat?" I purr at her. Kat rolls her eyes in response, but winks at me when no one's looking.

It's been a long time since we've been this close, and I can't stop the pull that makes me stand in front of the bar. She slides the beer over the top of the counter, and I take it from her, unable to stop from staring at her.

Kat busies herself by getting the brothers drinks, while Ghost and I start catching up right before I'm sure he hears what the rest of us can hear as well.

Is Axl really going at his girl behind the office door? My brother has a set of brass balls. The desk scrapes loudly from what sounds like it being pushed across the hardwood floor, along with moans from Dana in between.

Ghost grinds his teeth together, and I can't wait for that stupid ass to get out here and face her father. This really could not be more perfect.

"So, are you guys staying with Dana while you're here?" I look at Ghost, but he doesn't respond, so Katie, his Ol' Lady, chimes in. "Well, uh, I think we were, but maybe we may need a room." She nervously bites her lip, and I can't help but snicker.

She fills me in on all her activities in California while Ghost stares ahead. The banging in the office quiets down, and, shortly after, Axl emerges with Dana. I start clapping for the happy couple, then another clap is heard, and another, until the entire bar claps for their office sexcapade. Even Vegas, Jenn and Kat do it!

Dana's face turns a bright red and her eyes hit the floor when she sees her dad's arms are crossed over his chest with a very pissed off look on his face. Her mom has her hand over her mouth, trying to stifle her laugh when Ghost turns to glare at her instead of Axl.

I look over at Axl and see that he's not worried one bit as he smacks an '*I don't give a fuck your dad's here kiss*' on her lips. Shaking my head, I give my brother knuckles behind Dana's back and take a drink from my beer.

It doesn't take long for the brothers to take their Ol' Ladies home, the ones that have one anyway. And, then, the real party starts. Strippers, baby. I spared no expense and bought me, I mean Pawn and Solo and the guys, some working girls for our momentous occasion.

Putting two fingers to my mouth, I get their attention with a high-pitched whistle. "To mark this occasion, I have hired entertainment. First two lap dances go to Pawn and Solo."

The room fills in with strippers of all shapes and sizes, and, not to mention, different talents if asked. They're all from the local strip club.

I set up two chairs in the middle of the room, back-to-back, and whistle loudly to the brothers in case some of them missed the action walking in. Cowboy and Snake push Solo and Pawn into the two chairs. I laugh to myself and elbow Spider who's standing next to me.

A group of strippers come forward through the crowd, and the music changes to their bump and grind stripper mix they sent to Jenn. A couple of girls dance in front of Pawn and Solo, capturing their and everyone else's attention that's in the room.

A brave blonde straddles Pawn. His hands go up to grope her tits, but, before he gets too far, the girl off to the side handcuffs both of his hands to the chair, and he is scolded before she grinds around his body, thrusting her fingers into his hair.

Solo plays along and holds his hands up like he's being arrested, then he too is cuffed to his chair. The stripper in his lap whispers sweet nothings, how fucking cute, into his ear before giving him a little nip on his ear.

I would say lucky bastards, but, been there and done that. The guys enjoy the show and the girls spread the love, adding two more chairs for lap dances.

Sharp nails scratch across my back and shivers run up my spine. "You didn't call." Her nails scratch down my arm next, and I glance to my left.

I shrug a shoulder, "Didn't think you did these parties."

Topaz, their show stopper, stands in front of me with her bright blue eyes and long black hair. The bitch is fucking stunning. She runs her hands up the back of my neck and massages my scalp.

Fuck, she's trouble, and my dick springs to life for her. A better man might stop but a few memories of a few private nights we shared come forward, and she feels tempting.

"I've missed you, Tank," she purrs, her lips barely touching mine.

"Sorry, sweet cheeks, I have a party to host, I can't fuck around."

I pull my head up from her grasp and take a swig off my beer. She takes the hint and finds Spider to rub over for attention. He glares at her in disinterest. She scampers off quickly to save herself from another brush off. Poor Topaz, she's picking up on the wrong guys here.

"Cowboy," I call out and he backs up only to barely take his eyes off the two girls that are taking each other's tops off.

I nudge his shoulder and he turns around to face me. "See that girl over there?" He gives me a nod, and I pass him a stash of cash. "Go ask her to give you the Midnight Topaz special."

Cowboy bites his lip, and, before he can leave, I hold his shoulder, "Tell her she's a beautiful girl too, and don't forget your fucking manners." I let go and he is off, making me chuckle.

"I'm so happy. I feel proud of my boys, just look at this." I spread my arms wide before me with the beer in my hand. "I'm such a good host," I say to really anyone that would listen, because, aren't they all hearing me anyway?

Giggles and laughter fill the air for hours. I spend most of my time sitting next to that squirrely, mean bastard Spider. Nature hits me and I need to take a piss.

I leave the crowded bar scene and walk into the bathroom, letting out an ooooohhhh when I release the keg of beer I drank. It is that serious of a piss.

There's a moan behind me and I comment in support, "I know, buddy, let it out." Then, a giggle? What the hell.

I tuck my big dick away, zip up and turn around only to see Topaz bent over against the wall in the handicap bathroom stall. Cowboy pulls out and it's my cue to wash up and get out. The sounds of clothes being wrestled back on and murmurs of post fucking love making follow me all the way to the door.

The same time I'm ready to exit, I hold the door open for Topaz to leave because I'm a gentleman and shit. Keeping one hand on the wide-open door, I direct her out with the other, and she smiles, "Thank you, Tank."

I step out after her and see Kat standing in the hallway, staring at us. I push forward and pin her against the wall.

"Hey, baby, I've been waiting to get my hands on my K-Love again." I say it with all the honesty I have in me. I've missed the fuck out of her. Even when I was drunk, she was on my mind.

Kat's eyes radiate pain and anger so fierce, it scares me a bit.

"What happened?" I gently stroke her face and she rips out of my hold before she nails that big dick of mine with her knee, then takes off.

"Wha-t just happ-ened," I wheeze out, holding my stomach, crunched over.

I shuffle back inside the bathroom to puke into the toilet and lay there until I pass out from the pain, or beer, or both.

Fuckin' love hurts.

"Poke him harder," the voice above me demands before a pointed object digs into my ribs.

I roll over onto my side and cough on the cold concrete floor. "Toto, this isn't the clubhouse, is it?"

Laughter ensues and I crack an eye open to find Vegas and Blade staring me down while holding a broom. Vegas smiles and Blade looks less than pleased to inform me, "Spider said you never made it back to the club last night, but I didn't think we would find you here."

I moan from the brutal body aches I have all over and pull my body up and off the floor to sit against the wall. "Kat kneed me in the balls, and I passed out drunk after I puked," I explain as I'm rubbing the sleep from my eyes, then look up to see Blade still holding the broom and Vegas covering her mouth with one hand.

Blade groans and leans forward, offering me his hand to help me up. "Meet us in the bar."

They leave and I take care of business again, then walk out of the... ladies' room? Shit, I thought I crawled into the men's room last night. Thank God for small blessings from the man above, because, drunken men. Need I say more?

Walking out into the bar, I find the room crawling with brothers cleaning up from the night before, and now the broom makes so much more sense. I go straight to the bar and grab a cup of coffee and a donut before my interrogation in the office begins.

Vegas is sitting in a chair in front of her desk and Blade is in the desk chair. My, how things have turned around. I plop my sluggish heavy body into a chair and look at my executioner with my best puppy eyes, just in case. I really don't know if anything else happened last night that I don't know about because I had to leave my own party early. A big toothy grin overcomes my face at some of the memories.

"Wipe that smile off your face," Blade glares at me. "The bar is trashed, asshole, and you're staying until it's all cleaned up. Now, why the hell were you on the floor in the women's bathroom?"

I sigh and take a sip of coffee, then take a bite out of my donut while I try to retrace my steps from the night before.

"Sometime today, Tank." Blade stops me from pulling the memory with his outburst at me. I hold up my finger and close my eyes. It finally all comes back into place like a puzzle and my eyes pop open with it.

I look over to tell Vegas because she's easier to talk to. It feels like a good cop, bad cop type of situation in here, and I would rather look at the good cop while I tell this story.

When I'm done, it's Vegas who has a big toothy grin this time, and I don't dare a look over to Blade. It looks like he actually cracked a smile. "It was a good party, right? I don't get why Kat was so mad at me?!"

Blade shakes his head and slowly gives me the highlights of when Topaz ran her hand over my body and then us walking together out from the bathroom. And the final piece of that puzzle slams into place. "So, you're saying she loves me?"

"No one said anything about love, Tank," Vegas reasons, and I deflate, however, it doesn't mean that it's not true. "But, it looks like after whatever you two had together, it hurt her. That's a good start, if you can get her to believe you."

"I'm on it, no worries. She's mine." I take another sip of coffee and a bite out of my donut, not worried at all.

"Also, consider not letting other women, especially strippers and sluts, touch you, if you claim she's yours. Can men touch your woman?" Vegas raises a questioning brow.

All I can think is that, no, hell to the fucking no. No one can touch my woman, and I need to make it up to her.

CHAPTER 25

Tank

Well, those grand plans of redemption have been nearly impossible to execute. We buried one of our V.P.'s shortly after we patched Solo and Pawn in. Mad Max, who also happened to be Axl's father, was from the Las Vegas chapter. Axl went AWOL after losing his dad, and the club has been putting out fires left and right.

I, or anyone else for that matter, didn't see that shit coming. Morale has been down, and Kat has been gone. I don't know where, but I have a sinking feeling that Spider does, and I have a bargaining chip I think he'll bite into.

I find Spider at the clubhouse in his office, working, so I stroll in and shut the door. He rolls around, giving me his full attention.

"You want information on Jazz, and I may know someone who knows someone over in Cali."

Jazz is the cute little tattoo artist that is cousins with Vegas and comes up here every so often. Spider has been seen sniffing around her.

I wait for that to sync in. And since he doesn't say anything, I know that I am right. He's interested but doesn't want to be.

"I'll trade information with you for help."

"You want to know what I know about Kat?"

I nod at him and hope he bites. But now I have a feeling that he won't when he calmly asks, "So, you met her in Las Vegas, right, and hooked up, then she took off without a trace?"

"Yes, why do ask?"

Spider sighs, "Brother, she's not just Kat. She is more than I can tell you, but you don't know the real her. Isn't it odd that she lets you and everyone else call her a name *you* gave her? She hooked up with you in Las Vegas and now she's here like *ta-dah...*"

He gives me an exasperated look. "I know we've had our focus on all this other club shit, but it's time to open those eyes."

"In other words, you aren't going to tell me what you know yet, are you?"

I won't lie, it really bugs me that he doesn't want to share the information with me because we are brothers and we share everything, unless the club becomes the priority, in which case, she has importance that I don't know about.

I sit and think, and Spider turns back around while I mull over his words.

Moments pass before I word vomit my thoughts out loud. "She never hooked up with me. *I* hooked up with *her.* In fact, I skated in when she was working on banging the bartender that night. Kat never hustled me, Spider."

A part of me feels angry at him for implying that she used me like that. "She took off like she fucked up, and, since then, she has been avoiding me, not trying to pry information from me." This I know down to my core and no one can tell me otherwise. "But it says a lot about what you *didn't* say, which is that she's working for the club and that's why you're not telling me anything."

Who the fuck *is* this woman? My gut tells me that the answer may be my own hell, and that I better figure out if Kat is the woman for me, and fast. The answer to that is, fuck yeah, she is.

I'm coming for you, baby.

I take off from the clubhouse, on a mission to go find her and talk some sense into her for once. Somewhere where there isn't booze or bitches hanging around.

A smile creeps across my face as I think of the next person I can gather information from. The roar of my bike grabs the attention of the people standing around the lot. After parking, I go in search of the one person that I know without a doubt will help me.

Tami is working behind the bar, cleaning and prepping for later tonight. "Hey, Tami, where is everyone?"

She startles a bit, not having heard me walking into the bar, and waves, "Hey, Tank, Emilia just left to take

Vegas some stuff and should be back soon. It's just me for now. Why?"

"I was going to talk with Vegas," I sigh and settle onto the barstool in front of her.

"Can I help you with something?" God, she's sweet.

"I guess so, I need to take some stuff over to Kat's place, and I don't have her phone number or address. It'll have to wait I guess." I get up from the stool and move to leave before my little helper stops me.

"Hey, don't you remember that I moved in with her? She gave me her phone number, too. Hold on a minute, I'll send it and our address to you." She shuffles around from behind the bar, taking her phone out of her back pocket and sending me a few texts with the information.

I almost feel bad, but, nah, if Tami knew why, I'm sure she would be cool with it. I just don't want Kat to see me coming.

"Thanks, kid, I'll be back a little later." She gives me a shy wave in return, and I walk over to the Battle Born Tattoo to get to work.

I prep the young woman's hip and place a tattoo of flowers and a tiger to it with a stencil. She smiles down at me with hopeful eyes. Jesus, it's going to be a long day, I can feel it. A beautiful woman wants my attention, and, just a month ago, I would have really considered it, but that's changed. I need to figure this shit out with Kat, and soon. My dick has never been so trapped by one chick before.

It takes me a long eight hours at the shop and my hand feels tight with the workload. We've been behind on our appointments, so Blade and I usually work extra hours to catch up since Axl is still gone down in Las Vegas, and we try to cover his customers, too.

For a moment, I entertain the thought of asking Blade out right about Kat, but, since Spider already shut me out, I don't think he will budge either.

Gathering my phone and shutting off the light, I see a shadow barely noticeable outside through the lights of the room next to mine. Pulling out my gun from my desk drawer, I creep slowly outside and around the building.

I raise my hands, pointing the gun toward the shadow. With steady hands and light feet, I step quietly until I walk up behind the person slinking against the building.

"Hello, *wife*."

Ever so slowly, Kat turns around and smiles at me before wiping the happy off her face. "Why are you sneaking up on me with a loaded gun?"

"Why are you walking around and spying in the shadows?" I counter, then tuck the gun back behind my back. I really start wondering if I've been sleeping with the enemy all along. What kind of woman creeps around in the shadows like a damn psychopath?

"I'm not your wife."

"I think you *could* be after our night in Vegas. I was wasted enough to not remember much the next day. I'm starting to believe that my *wife* drugged me that night and took advantage of me in more ways than one."

My head tilts to the side as I look over what she's wearing. Full black clothing to hide in the shadows, but what for? Is she looking for something, or hiding from it?

Arrogance covers her face, showing the mask of who she really is, the person she wants me to see. "No, Tank, we never made it to a chapel that night, a room only."

I step closer, caging her into the wall. "I don't know who you are, Kat, or your real name, but you and I are going to talk this out, what's between us."

Kat huffs at the words spoken. "There isn't shit that needs to be worked out." She goes to move, and I step in her way, placing a hand on the wall next to her shoulder.

"I didn't fuck around with any bitches, or Topaz, the night at the patch-in party. I took a piss and Cowboy was screwing her in the bathroom. Believe it or not, I'm not going to grovel at your feet for forgiveness, cupcake."

The woman glares at me and doesn't say a word. Her eyes go back and forth, indecision, then resignation dawning in them.

I push back and cross my arms over my chest. "Life is a calculated risk, never a guarantee. Tell me your name. Who *are* you?"

She shakes her head no. "No one knows my name, only a few, and there is a reason for it that I won't share with anyone on this earth until I'm ready."

"You are going to need to trust someone eventually, Kat. These secrets that you hold close have an expiration date, all of them do."

I lean in close, my eyes capturing hers. "I want to see what this is between us, but I'm not waiting forever for you either. *That* has an expiration date, too." I push off the wall and walk away, letting Kat go back to her spying or the recon she was doing in the shadows of the night.

Everyone has ties to something or someone, and there are files of it at the clubhouse. She's tied someway to the Battle Born if she's here.

I'm crazy just enough to find out what it is and who she really is.

Kat

"You're making shit worse by acting incognito, you know that, right?" Spider startles me as he steps out from behind the building on the opposite side.

"You thought Tank was a stupid fucker and you could get away with a fuck and run. The man is the Road Captain for a reason." Spider walks closer to me. "I know who you are, Black Widow. Blade does, too, for now, and it's a matter of time before the entire club finds out the full extent of the problem we have."

"You were supposed to keep Tank busy so I could work," I scowl back, my pride winning over the disappointment I have over my weakness for Tank.

His maniacal chuckle fills the air. "He's been busy because the club kept him that way. Tank's right, you're going to drown in your secrets soon. Make a choice if you are going to work with us or hold on to them. Eventually, they will look like lies."

Spider steps a little closer and drills me with a look I've seen on many faces before him, death. "I will protect my family from you if it comes to that. Don't keep demanding secret meetings from me. Here on out, you will meet me on my terms and start helping if you want the fuck out alive, for now."

My damn pride and my past I hold so close make me choke on doubt. Trusting this MC with my life and with others' that are more important than my own is everything.

Spider waits for me to decide, and I am well aware that my decision will affect the future. If I had a crystal ball or a something to guide me, that would be so helpful. I do what I always do and choose based on what my head and heart tell me. The heart that others can't see under the guns, tattoos and courage.

"Now that I helped you kill the cop that Axl ran off the road, and he's long gone, you are right. It's time to move forward. But this is a conversation that your Prez needs to hear in person."

Spider points to the building, signaling for me to follow him. Together, we walk into the tattoo shop where Blade is cleaning his room after finishing up with his last client. The space is empty of other people. Even Sunshine, the receptionist, is long gone. Spider locks the front door behind me as soon as I walk into the shop.

He does a sweep of the rooms while Blade and I take a seat and wait for him. Blade's stone face remains impassive as he lights a smoke from the pack waiting on his desk. Spider comes back into the room and sits on the edge of his tattoo chair. "Kat has made her choice." He then looks me in the eyes. "Go ahead, let's hear it."

Taking a deep breath, I start from the beginning. "I'm the daughter of the Mexican MC Prez of the the Cursed Kings, *Los Malditos Reyes* MC. I was raised to be a prize that was to be married off just like Cuervo's wife, before she died."

I can't help feeling the pain, and my true accent creeps out with every word.

"Before I go any further, it's important that you should know, if my true identity comes out too early, you will engage in another war just from me sitting here with you."

Blade takes a long drag, and, on an exhale, he sees through my words when he says, "It's not your father, the Prez, you are hiding from. Who is it?"

Taking his question as his understanding of what I said, I take a deep breath and continue. "I'm the wife of the Mexican Cartel boss. Matias is my husband." The words hang in the air between us three like a death sentence.

"My mother was best friends with Cuervo's wife, Rosa. When I was a kid, she would take my sister and me to visit her. I never knew who Rosa was because my father, Cobra, had forbidden my mother to see her. She was just a friend to my mother as far as I was concerned. I never knew who it was I had visited until I left Mexico and started putting everything together." For a solid year I investigated as much as I could of my family and who they were. "Rosa was my aunt, a sister to my father.

"Rosa was supposed to marry Matias' father when he was the boss. That didn't work out as you already know, so Cobra killed her and then my mother after she found out what my father had been planning to do with me. Marry me off to the Cartel boss' son. She was going to run with me, and he killed her while she was trying to save my sister and me."

"Why did you leave your husband?" Spider questions, and I can see the mistrust in his stare.

"Personal reasons only. I can't share that piece until he is dead. One of us will have to die at the end of this. I am highly hopeful that it will be Matias."

Blade runs a hand over his scruffy face. "What does Cobra have to do with the Cartel? He obviously traded you for something."

I get up from my spot and walk to the window because I can't show them the honesty on my face.

"I loved Matias once. When you grow up in the life, the things that happen seem normal, because it is *your* normal. I was given to Matias as a bargaining chip, or an alliance. My father was to mule drugs, women and children for the Cartel over the border."

My spine straightens now that I'm done getting through the first half of my story, and I turn to face them. "They needed your territory, or rather Stryker's, to get what they needed done. Matias schemed behind his father's back to do two things, kill his father to take his place as boss, and start a club war."

Taking a small breath, I finish the rest of the story. "Matias manipulated Cobra and Stryker into the war to get what he wanted. Matias made it look like Cobra was hauling through your territory. Then he ordered a hit on Cobra's man while in Las Vegas to piss Cobra off, and hauled the cargo back before either of you could locate it. It looked like you killed his man, so Cobra came after your MC. With the bad blood between Battle Born and *Los Reyes Malditos* already happening after the killing of Cuervo's wife, the entire thing was easily manipulated. As soon as the war broke out, I took the opportunity to get out of Mexico and as far from Matias as I could."

Blade and Spider sit with the heavy cloud of lies and betrayal still keeping them from seeing the truth. "How can we trust you that Matias didn't send you to sabotage the MC and take the northern territory as their own like they planned all along?"

"I have documents I can show you that I stole from him before I left, but you and I both know that's bullshit. I do know that Johnny is being paid by the Cartel to maneuver the shipments for them. Cobra couldn't get the job done so they moved in up here and tried to worm in through the old Prez and Johnny." I take an exhale and hold Spider's gaze. "You can spin whatever you want on paper, right, Spider?"

"I wouldn't believe it even on paper."

"You asked for trust from me and I have to ask for the same from you. This is my plan. I am going to take Matias down, one pillar at a time. I'm taking out key men working under him and weaken his resources before I go after him."

Blade stubs out his smoke and bends forward, resting his forearms on his knees. "You could die, Kat. I don't know that the club will back you indefinitely."

It's not a surprise to me to hear those words. I was expecting them.

"I know that, Blade. Even though Cuervo is my uncle, Vegas and Jenn my cousins, I'm under no illusion that I am your MC family. We only have a mutual problem, and that is Cobra and the Cartel. I want them both dead. I can't be the one to kill Cobra. Matias will know it was me and he will come. It is too soon."

What I am asking is a lot. If they fail, their club goes back to war.

"He is the one behind your past Prez transporting the diamonds and kids through here. Cobra and Matias won't stop until they get what they want. If we don't take them both down, Matias will keep sending people until he wins, and you will never know who's coming after you, after your family."

"There is only one thing I know for a fact, and that is, Tony and Cobra have to die." Blade gives me a lethal look, and, with a deadly sneer, he stands.

"You fuck me over, and you will know what it's like to be hunted and skinned alive."

CHAPTER 26

Tank

Waltzing into Kat and Tami's house, I get a feel of their bare surroundings. Well, not exactly waltzing, more like breaking and entering, but I'm on a mission none the less.

If I were a secret hiding spot... I think Kat is going to have a stellar hideaway location for her most precious items. Probably her room where she has control over the environment and can remember where every last item was placed.

Hours go by and I'm on the verge of giving up. There are just bare bones in this place. Nothing identifying Kat or Tami. They have done well concealing their identities. It dawns on me that Kat may never store anything here. She could have a separate hiding spot, and even never in the same place for too long.

I do know that she doesn't have the company of a man too often with the vibrator she has stored in her dresser. Flicking it on, I chuckle to myself. She must have put new batteries in this guy. I can only imagine the miles she puts on it.

Against my better judgement of stealing it, I place it back in the drawer. She would be one pissed off woman if she didn't have her plastic toy to take the edge off. Another time.

There is nothing of importance in the house, which tells me that the woman has an alternate location. It's time for the Road Dog to make some business decisions.

I leave her house and, as I come up over the hill, I decide that Solo and Pawn will be placed on stalk Kat duty.

On my ride back to the clubhouse, I formulate my plan. My mind is buzzing by the time I get to The Black Rose. I walk into the bar and find the guys I need to talk to first. As I explain their top-notch secret mission, they both grimace, and for good reason.

Pointing a finger into their faces, I growl at them. "Don't fucking cry about it. At least you can go to the bar and take turns staring at Tami while the other one waits to tail Kat home."

Neither one wants to argue with me, I am the reason they are standing here.

"Got it, we'll let you know what we find," Pawn gives in first. He's just pissed because this will cut into their free time to fuck and smoke. Yeah, I feel you, my dick is sad, too. The sooner we solve the Kat mystery, the sooner we all get a boner a woman will take care of.

"Glad you see this my way. Don't forget, if you fuck up, we are fucking toast with Blade and I can't guarantee your safety with Kat," I shrug.

I'm not entirely sure she wouldn't put a bullet in their heads to protect her secrets and Blade won't give each of us a mother of all beat downs. Risky business falling in love.

Solo's head tilts a little at that last comment. "Are you kidding right now?" he whispers under his breath so that the others don't overhear.

"She is a mystery." And that makes me laugh because ain't that the fucking truth.

Next, I text the V.P. of dicks, Axl, and let him know that I'll be running home for a few days, to California, and that I'm stopping by to see Fuego, the California MC chapter Prez. He doesn't respond right away, and I don't figure that he will. He just got back from Las Vegas and he's patching shit up with his Ol'Lady.

As I'm packing my shit for my trip, I feel an urgency to get this handled, and I can't explain if it is because of Kat or because of a need to protect the MC. I do know, though, for some unanswered reason, that my mind knows I'm headed down the right road.

I stuff what I need in my saddle bags and hit the open road. That's where the Road Dog is at home.

I fly freely down the highway, over the mountain pass and through Lake Tahoe, taking the scenic route and letting my mind wonder. I realize that at the end of this trip, I may not find the answers I want, but the ones that are needed none the less.

Soon enough, as it's getting close to dawn, I roll into the parking lot of the Battle Born MC clubhouse in California. This place has been here for about as long as the one in Las Vegas. Fuego meets me at the front door since I let him know I was on my way.

"Tank, *ven a dentro*," he greets me with a wide-awake smile. I must be tired as fuck because I have no idea what he just said. I follow him to his office, and he's holding a cup of coffee in one hand and a shot of tequila in the other, my pick.

I can't help but laugh. I miss this asshole and it's a test to see why I'm here. I take the tequila. He then laughs and walks around his desk, taking the coffee with him as he goes to sit in his chair. "*Que pasa, mijo?*"

After another shot, I tell my friend, brother and a man that I look up to, everything that has happened with Kat. I even tell him about what Spider told me. "She's connected to the club. I just don't know how yet and what the secrets are for."

"Hmm, depends, *mijo*, is she protecting herself for good or bad reasons? Only time will tell. What does she look like? Describe her to me."

I tell him everything I know, and, even with my foggy mind, I wonder out loud, "Do you know her?"

"Possibly, Tank. Does Blade know who she is?"

"I think so because they are holding this situation close until things are handled."

Fuego sets the coffee down and trades it for a shot of tequila instead. "This is bigger than I thought possible. Trust your Prez that he is making the correct choice for us all."

He rambles for a few moments before looking off into the distance. "You know the story of how Cuervo lost his wife, yes?"

Instantly, my mind sobers and wakes up, enraptured by the story.

"Rosa, she had a beautiful sister-in-law, she was married to Cobra. He killed her shortly after the death of Rosa for running away from him. She had two daughters. He kept the *niñas* and married one off to the Cartel later. It's rumored the man kept them both as his, but—" He stops to prop his cowboy boots up on the desk. "One of them ran away and became what is known as the Black Widow. She lives in the shadows, waiting for the revenge, to kill the men she wants most, her father and her husband. She sounds like a *fantasma*, no?"

"Sure."

Fuego laughs, "A ghost, Tank."

"A ghost, yes, I would definitely describe her as a ghost. I don't understand, how do they not know if she is gone?"

Fuego smirks, "You would think that would be easy to answer. The reason it is hard to know the truth is, they're sisters, identical twins. The *jefe*, Matias, if he kept them both, who would know which one which? If she is here, she is declaring a war against her husband. A battle to the death. No one leaves a Cartel boss and lives to breathe long enough to tell the stories. If his people found the truth, it would shame him greatly. He wants her dead."

I sink back in my chair and legit cannot grab a hold of one feeling long enough to know what to do with it. Angry that she's married. And she was mad at *me* for the situation with Topaz when she's *married*? Sadness because she *is* married. Pissed off at the whole damn thing and just plain confused as fuck with this twisted tale.

"This is just a story, Tank, we don't know if it is fact, yet. But that would make her Cuervo's niece."

"What is her name?"

"Katherine Castillo."

I pull up my phone and google her name. That's when her picture appears before me. My eyes memorize every detail of it. It's her but without a trace of any tattoos on her skin. I check the date of the charity event this was taken at, and it can't be her, it is too recent. So, in fact, Kat or Katherine, is a twin living a double life it seems.

I hand my phone over to Fuego and he looks at the picture, "This her?"

"No, that's her twin. The Black Widow is real and full of tattoos."

"The stories, there's always a small piece of truth in them, but not a hundred percent. What are you doing next?" Fuego asks and sets his feet down on the floor.

"I'm going to sleep a few hours and hit the road south until I find out everything I can."

Fuego has a couch in his office, I stand and stretch my sore body before lying down to catch a nap.

"Does this woman, the Black Widow, or Kat, as you call her, does she haunt you? Is this why you are here?"

I smile at my brother, "*Sí*, Fuego, she haunts the fuck out of me, and I need to know everything about her, and I don't have a clue why."

"None of us do, *mijo*, when we find our woman." Fuego gets up and walks to the door. "Be careful, *mijo*, know I'm on your team, yeah?"

"Yeah, team building and shit."

Fuego shakes his head and leaves me to sleep and have haunted dreams of the woman I can't get out of my head.

It feels like I just closed my eyes when there's something poking me again, and I swat at it with one hand. My ribs are jabbed again but much harder this time.

"What in the fuck!" I roar and jump up to stand over a tiny little Hispanic woman with a big smile on her face. Closing my eyes, I take a calming breath before I hurt this cute little thing, and run my hands over my face.

"*Ve a bañarte mientras te lavo la ropa, sí?*"

I stand there and blink, then blink again. She repeats herself and I just stand there, and we stare at each other.

"She wants you to go shower and she'll wash your clothes for you." Hawk walks into the room from the doorway and helps to translate. "Most guys here speak Spanish, or they learn quickly."

"*Ve, y te conseguiré un plato para cuando vuelvas,*" she says, and I look over at Hawk. "Go shower and she'll get you a plate of food, too," he explains for her.

I'm about to argue that I need to get going, and I open my mouth to say so, but the five-foot nothing woman scowls at me, and, if I ever want to come back, I need to think better of it.

She walks past, knowing I will do as she asked, then looks at Hawk, "*Cabróne.*"

"What did she say?"

"Oh, she just called me a fucker. Vegas' grandmother." Hawk brushes it off like it's happened a lot over the years. I wouldn't doubt that it has since he cheated on Vegas when they were married and then she left the state. In the grandma's eyes he's responsible for taking the granddaughter away from her.

After I shower, I patiently wait at the table for who everyone in this house calls *abuela*, or grandma, to dry my clothes. She's like the house nanny, housekeeper, cook and nemesis to Hawk. Way better than the club sluts. In fact, I see none. She must keep them away when she's around. I would take her home to Nevada if I didn't think Fuego would kill me for her.

Abuela places in front of me a heaping plate of beans, rice and some kind of meat with green sauce and a stack of hot tortillas. "*Comer, niño.*"

"*Gracias, abuela.*" I pick up a fork and she chuckles at me, then goes back to cleaning, leaving us to eat.

I look over to Fuego and see that he's digging in using only his tortillas that are ripped in half, and then again as he picks up the food. He pinches the food underneath with the tortilla and shoves it into his mouth a bite at a time. This confuses me, hence why I am sure she left me a fork, so I make tacos, eating my food the only way I know how.

It's a few beers later when she presents to me my perfectly laundered clothes. They smell so good. I pull the stack she offered me up to my nose and get down on one knee. "Come home to *mi casa* at the clubhouse, *abuela*," I propose.

"*Que seas bien*, may you be good." She pats my head and I hold my hand to my heart like she broke it, and laugh. "Women." I brush it off and shake hands with Fuego and a few of his men, including Hawk. The bastard now has a club bunny perched on his lap.

I'm back on the road a few hours later than I wanted but headed south to talk to a few contacts. By the time I'm in south California, I pull up every marker for information and hunt down every man that has ever owed me a favor.

Within hours, I find the biggest secret and why Kat is doing this. I sit outside a house with a very homey feel to it, and watch a family play in the yard. My heart hurts for this woman and what she has done to protect it.

After I confirm the marker I collected for information was true, I get back on the road and find the man that sent me the information. He said he would meet me, but he would also collect a ten-thousand-dollar fee on top of what he had already been paid. My mind races, because, if he sold the location of this family to me, then he more than likely would or *has* sold it to others already.

In a crowded bar in downtown Lodi, I park my bike down the block and leave my cut in the saddle bag to go meet my source. The dickhead smirks at me when I enter. Walking in, I mask my fury and give him my best smile, but, inside, the rage I feel for this asshole sizzles beneath the surface.

We grab some beers like old friends, and I finally ask, "How did you find that information on the family? Before I hand over ten grand, I want to know I am the only one with this information."

"I worked under a man that helped falsify documents, you know, green cards and birth certificates and such. This hot Latina walked in needing information and work done."

He takes a drink of his beer and, setting the mug down, he explains, "About a year ago, a man came in dressed hella slick and was asking about a woman that looked like the woman I saw but not the same. I knew one day someone would come asking, and here we are."

"Did the man tell them about her?"

"They asked all the wrong questions, they were looking only for her. So, it was easy for him to lie and say no. My boss doesn't give out information, if word got out, he wouldn't have a business. You are the only one that knows."

There's a good possibility that this little puke fuck told someone else, but, being he's still breathing, we may be lucky. "Thanks, man, my boss will be happy. I have the money out in my car."

The little prick gets up and follows me out to the back door, making my life easy. "You parked back here?" he comments and looks left, then right, in the dark alley that's full of dumpsters.

"Oh shit, you're right, let's walk out front." He steps in front of me and heads toward the street. I pull the nine-millimeter out that already has a silencer on and put a few bullets into his back. He gasps and falls over as blood bubbles up from his mouth, leaking out onto the pavement. Kneeling, I take his wallet and cellphone with me on my long ride home.

Spider and I are having a come to fucking Jesus moment when I get back.

CHAPTER 27

Kat

The loneliness that usually haunts me resides as a deeply rooted ache in my chest, but, lately, even more so than it usually does.

Looking around the bar, I see that there are happy couples or young and single people, so carefree, never having the life experiences that usually pull you under with their weight. Is it because I haven't talked with Tank for weeks? I don't know for sure, but it is not the only reason today feels worse than usual.

It's better that I don't know what it's like to have him around me. I can barely breathe, the ache in my chest is so severe that it's crippling me. Each thought is just as more unbearable, if not more, than the next when my mind sweeps me back into a time. The most bittersweet moment of my existence.

My stomach is overgrown with my beautiful child inside. I know the baby is a boy. I can feel it, the truth as clear as the water in the glass next to me. My hand runs over my large stomach, knowing that my time of peace is about up, and I want to cry. My heart wants to give in already.

I want to take my little boy and run far away with him, into another life. I have to move on, though, for him and no one else. He saved my life, I know he did. He woke me up and made me see the reality of my life and the position I was in.

His foot pushes back on my hand with a kick, and I smile through the tears. He feels me just like I feel him.

He may have been gifted to me for all the wrong reasons, but he is all the right ones in my world. Had he not come when he did, I would have stayed and grown darker into the world I was raised in.

I will always love the man I thought his father to be, but not the man that he is.

My hand jumps back with another kick and I hold it there. I hold onto these precious moments because Jane gets to be his mother. She will feed him, kiss and hug him when he's hurt, and not me. I want those things more than any power in the world. I want him.

Tears stream down my face with a bittersweet calmness. It's not fair but it is what has to be done to protect him.

"I love you, Eli," I rasp and choke on the words as I'm swinging back and forth on the porch swing. "One day, baby, you and I, even if it is not meant for this world but the next."

My eyes clench shut, and I take deep breaths in until my body relaxes. I memorize the feel of him, the sweet smell of the late summer air, and the slight chill of it. I tuck this moment away for forever, locking it away in memory. A small gift. I had it all for a short time.

I know time is up when my body clenches with a sharp pain that starts in my back and radiates around the front of my stomach. Calmly, I absorb everything and breathe through each and every contraction through the night.

I sit alone, not wanting anyone to disturb my last few moments of perfection.

Hours must pass before I finally wake Jane up and she helps to situate me on the bed, along with her supplies. It takes me several agonizing pushes with sweat that pours from me, drenching the sheets around me.

At four-twenty-four in the morning, a cry from my son pierces the air with his strong lungs for the first time.

After he is cleaned, I hold him to me for a few hours before I have to leave.

A beer bottle breaking in the distance wakes me from my trance behind the bar. Tami rushes over to clean up after the accident and I look away, back to cutting limes and begging the memories to leave me be for today.

I look around and wonder if any of these people are drowning in their own pain like I am. They sure don't show it. Not like me, and not like today.

My throat constricts because I missed another one of Eli's birthdays. I sent him a gift, but it is not the same, and it's in no way good enough for him.

Vegas comes in carrying some books for the office and walks past the bar, smiling. My mind and emotions clam up and I hide them away from the world and her to see.

"*Hola, chica!*" She must have already dropped the books off on her desk along with the rest of her things, because, all of a sudden, she is right across from me, looking me square in the eyes as she comes around to stand in front of me. "Shots or coffee?"

My eyes dart back in forth over her face. "Are you asking me what you should drink?"

"Nah, you don't have your usual *'I kill for fun'* sparkle. It's a little more like, *'fuck, someone kill me already'* gloom and doom. What's going on?" She tilts her head a little to the side and patiently waits me out.

I'm feeling broken and alone, and if I wasn't so stuck in my head, I could move past this already.

"It has just been a hard life, Vegas."

I used to have my sister to talk to, and that's laughable because she was fucking my husband and I doubt she loved me at all.

"Mmm. I think it's a shots kind of conversation. How about this then," she pulls me around the bar and sits me in the barstool, then walks back around the bar. "I'm just nobody, a bartender, tell me anything you want. I've heard them all and I don't care what you have to say."

Vegas waits for me to respond, and I want to say yes, but I can't tell her anything because she can't be dragged into this. I want and need more than anything to have a friend or a sister to vent to. I miss my mother so much right now.

I'm pretty sure Vegas' man will skin me alive like he promised he would if I mutter one word. I wouldn't blame him. It would be selfish of me to tell her my story and put her at risk, because I know that she'd come in swinging.

She grabs a bottle of Tequila Rose off the top shelf, strawberry cream liqueur and black vodka. "We only make these for special guests." She winks at me and passes me over a pink shot swirled with the black vodka. "These will tear you from the floor up, or put you down on the floor, you know what I'm saying?" She clinks her glass to mine. "To love, family and finding yourself with those you love. *Salud*."

"*Salud*," the word comes out raw and graveling from the tears that I hide behind my eyelids when I tip my head back to pour the shot down my throat. *Happy birthday, baby boy*, I say in my head, feeling even more alone, and slam the glass on the countertop.

Vegas sees the pain I can't blink away, not today. I open my mouth to say something when the front door opens, shutting down any conversation immediately.

Tank strolls in with Spider in tow, with a look on his face that I've never seen before. The face of a killer or boss of the man that belongs to the MC, and not the lover who gave himself over to me. This is who he truly is.

I get up from the stool and walk over to the main floor where I start sliding chairs from the tabletops to the floor.

Quietly, the three of them talk, discussing business while I try to pretend that he's not here. Their conversation stops and the bar grows quiet as their footsteps take them behind Vegas' closed door of her office.

I contemplate running and getting the hell out of here. My skin crawls with the anxiety of staying in the same building as Tank. It's too much today with everything else. I can't be strong and hide what is killing me like cancer, painfully slow. The rawness will shine through.

I can't run, though, and the sinking feeling of being trapped like I was before increases. The memories of Matias start resurfacing and taking me under their dark cloud.

A hand wraps around my neck and I blink awake, clawing at his arms until I realize it's him. Matias. His other hand rips and tears my underwear down my legs, the only sound to be heard in the room other than his heavy breathing.

The burn from my skin ripping around the fabric left behind leaves tears in my eyes. His dick invades me and pushes through my flesh until he is seated, then starts rocking in and out of me. He pushes harder this time, and his hand squeezes my neck with more force, his greed of dominance taking full control of him.

He lets go for a moment to hover over me and hisses centimeters away from my face, "She's my whore, you are my wife. Know your place, Katherine."

A hand slices across my cheek and I hold back a scream from the blow. "Don't fucking make a scene again." Another hit on the other side of my face this time. "Can you smell her pussy on me?" he seethes, and I can't hold it back anymore.

I release the river of emotions I was trying to hold back. My heart tears in two and tears shed.

"Go fuck your dirty whore then, if I mean nothing to you." I pull his handgun out from his pants and hold it under my chin.

"Kat!"

A hand wraps around my arm, jolting me from my daydream and causing me to drop the chair. It clatters loudly to the floor. Tank backs up, holding both hands up in the air. "I was just trying to get your attention."

"Don't fucking touch me," I caution him, dropping my voice low. I take another step back when he comes closer. My mind races with the emotion, and, on instinct, I pull out the small handgun that's hidden under my shirt.

I feel exposed, raw, and wanting to hide and protect myself. I point the gun to his face, "Don't think you can ever touch me, Tank, no man owns me."

Surprise replaces the look of confusion he had earlier, and then sympathy, and I hate it. I hate that I opened myself up for this.

"Sorry, I won't do that again. Can you not point a loaded gun to my face though?" He's deadly calm along with the usual bustle of the bar.

"Kat," Vegas calls me from the side. "He's fucking stupid, okay? It's just Tank." She tries to coax me and steps closer. "Sometimes he doesn't know any other way than to bulldoze his way through. You know Tank..."

I look between them and slowly start to lower my hands and put the gun back into the side holster under my shirt. Taking in a deep breath, I try to focus on my breathing and calm my racing heart and heaving chest.

"Can we talk for a minute, Kat?" Tank appears more like the man I know, but I can't believe him. He has another woman, and he will turn on me.

"No need, we are fine," I grit out because a part of me misses his nicknames for me, and I hate that. I can't let him do what Matias did, constantly playing games with my mind and heart.

Cold, I have to be cold. Lock down these feelings.

I push around him and get back to the bar to finish my shift. Thankfully, Tami walks in from the back all smiles and perks up a bit at the sight of Tank.

"Hi."

She then greets everyone else that had arrived with him. They all respond but me, and I duck down to grab some glasses and pretend that I didn't hear her.

Tank gives her a hug and comments how much she's grown up in the last few months, treating her like the kid sister he's never had. A part of me, the really fucking fucked up in the head part, is jealous of her. How she gets a fresh start. Even though I am happy for her and happy to help her, I wish I could start over too.

Life is such a fucking whore, just like the assholes who fuck us over and play games.

Tank

I'm not sure what the hell happened with Kat, but it's pretty obvious that I fucked up again. I always seem to do that when it comes to her.

I didn't know the woman that I fucked in Las Vegas *or* the woman that I fucked months ago at the clubhouse.

Since finding out that she's married and comes with a fuckload of problems, I've kept away to sort my head out. Maybe it had something to do with my own past, but I didn't want to admit it could. I'm Tank, the laughing, funny asshole. He's easier for me to handle than the man who loves a woman who could love someone else, then leave me again, or my parents.

When I just walked into the bar, it came crashing down on me that she couldn't be mine like I thought.

There is no chance of us and that's why she made it clear there would not be an us.

Yep, I really fucked up when I grabbed her arm like she belonged to me, and she dropped the chair like I was about to kill her with my bare hands.

This chick is a whole other level of crazy, more so than I realized. Well, that's a little mean, but still true.

Now, I'm sitting in Vegas' living room, waiting for her and Blade to get home, drinking a six pack all by myself. When did this happen to me? When did this become my life?

A thud echoes against the door before giggles come through from the other side of it. I left it unlocked so the sound of the keys hitting the concrete makes me smile. I get up from the couch and swing the door open wide to my Prez making out with his woman on the front porch.

"You two kids are way past curfew. Vegas, get your ass to your room, you're grounded." I stand in the doorway with my hands on my hips.

Vegas tears her face away from Blade's to scowl at me, "Why are you in my house?"

Blade doesn't look pleased either, and he stands up to adjust his dick. "Go."

"I can't, I'm homeless. Dana doesn't need me anymore either since Axl is back."

All that is true, except that I *do* have a room at the clubhouse. And sitting around a bunch of assholes while wanting to punch one of them in the face sounds great, but really isn't. Truth is, I feel fucking alone there and that doesn't sit well with me.

"What is it, Tank?" Blade gets down to business and Vegas follows him into the living room where I have a mess of food and beer scattered. Her face turns red, and, to her credit, holds it in. That's why I love her, she knows when to blow up and when not to.

"I fucked up with Kat, and then, that doesn't even matter because she's married anyway, and this whole fucking thing is a mess."

I sit down and hand each of them a beer. Vegas takes hers, then hands one over to her Ol' Man, sitting down next to him and wrapping herself around him as much as possible. It sucks to see, especially when Blade lays a possessive hand on her thigh.

"What is it you want, Tank?" Blade cuts out all the B.S. in between.

"I want her, but I can't have her at all. She's some badass, crazy, gun wielding, vengeful woman, and married at that. I can't have her."

"I don't see why not," Blade bluntly states.

"Vegas, I don't get how he's not getting what I'm saying here."

She smirks and lowers her beer. "I think what he's saying, Tank, is that you can have whatever you want. You want Kat, then fight for her."

These two are confusing. "She's *marr-ieeed*, and to the *Cartel*!" I throw up my hands to further demonstrate my point.

"For fuck's sake, Tank, kill her husband and then she won't be married anymore. You can also fucking take her, and she can still be married. I *have* heard of men fucking married women before." He pauses to give me a pointed look. "I don't think that in her head she's actually married though, if you need permission. You two have already fucked." He gives me another stupid look, like I'm a dumbass.

"Whether Vegas was married or not, I was taking her, and I wouldn't have given a fuck about it because she was mine. Fucking take what you want or sit around and talk with us about your feelings some more. What's it gonna be? Fucking or feelings? You can't have both. Now get the fuck out."

He sets his beer down on the coffee table and scoops Vegas up, hauling her down the hallway before slamming their bedroom door.

"Good team building meeting, guys." I hold up my beer in my own little toast to myself and chug the rest of it before lying down and covering my head with a pillow to block out the fucking love making coming from the other room.

Tomorrow, I promise myself, I will do better and figure this one out.

CHAPTER 28

Tank

The words float in my head while I'm working in the garage the next morning. Team building.

The disappointment from the last few months has been daunting. Why did we have so much piled on the club when we did, and how did we get through it all? Together. We did everything as a team and didn't hesitate to pitch in even when it strained other relationships. We hung on *together*.

I'm not the smartest man, but I am the bravest and most honest I can be.

Deciding to take a break, I drop the wrenches and go in search of some quiet, along with, hopefully, some answers. Spider is in the kitchen grabbing a cup a coffee, and he hands me a pink mug with a straight face.

God only knows how it ended up here but I'm down to raise to his challenge. Filling it full, we sit down in quiet contemplation. For Spider, it's pretty normal. For me, it's not.

My hands fidget with first my cut, then my mug, twirling it around. Spider glares at me over his own mug while taking a loud sip. Jesus, he needs some manners, but I don't mention it. I don't have it in me, especially if I need his help.

A piece of me feels conflicted and lost. The Road Dog is lost on his journey. Go figure. To break the silence, I ask, "Did you check that dickhead's phone and internet records to see if he sold any information on Kat's family in California?"

"As far back as I could, but that's not a guarantee. What do you want me to do?" Spider asks, setting his mug down on the table in front of him. "I'm searching the best I can to find out who they all are to her. I think we need to put that on hold and find out who this little prick was working with under the radar."

I understand why he would say that but, "We need to relocate them too, and hide their identity. Which will be tricky, but let me think on it, and I'll come up with a plan."

I'm not saying no. He has a point to wait, I'm just not sure why I'm doing this. Going through all this trouble when I'm nothing to her.

We sit together for a bit longer before Spider leans forward. "What is it, Tank? What are you stuck on?"

"I don't even know. We fucked a few times, but I want more." Setting down my drink, I run my hands through my hair. "I don't think she gives two fucks about me though. Never had this reaction before and it's got my dick all twisted. And let me tell you, backed up blue balls is the lowest of low."

Spider barely cracks a smirk. "Why can't you have something less complicated with her for now?"

"That's what I think Blade was trying to say, but I don't know why I am not pursuing it harder. It pissed me off when she questioned me, when I found out who she really was, that she's married, and now this anonymous little tip about this unknown family..."

"You got to let the past go, Tank. Kat isn't your past. She's not the cute little college girl you were going to marry all those years ago and have a cute little family with, only to find out that she was only fucking you, and you were the other guy."

I know he's right, but it makes the unknown a scary place, sitting on the other end. She knows exactly who I am.

He takes a breath before continuing, "Her case is a lot more complicated. She told us from the beginning that she would only tell us what she could, when she was ready, for a reason. She's hiding but not from you. Faith, brother, learn to have faith."

Spider taps my shoulder on his way out, leaving me alone with yet more questions than answers.

Throughout my work day, I think about everything and every piece of wisdom shared with me, and let it all percolate. Unfortunately, by the time I'm ready to leave, we all get called into Church. More shit has gone down, more drama to deal with and handle. Solo and

Pawn follow me into the meeting room, and we all take a seat.

Blade and Axl take a call-in meeting from Fuego, then conference in the Elko and Las Vegas chapters. Fuego's voice sounds low and broken as he tells the clubs where Jenn has been and why. She tried to kill herself because of the club. Jenn was raped during the club war and she held it in to protect us all. The girl took one for the team when she shouldn't have had to.

All heads in the room hang from the pain she has endured alone all this time. None of us protected her or realized that she needed help. What if it was too late and she *would* succeed in killing herself?

James, Axl and Blade wrestle with themselves as they try to hold in the anger. We all agree to protect her, and avenge her, and be a hundred percent on her side to see this through.

It's fucked up, I know, but it comes to me that Kat is too holding in her own extreme pain and protecting everyone against all odds. And she doesn't have a single person to protect her. Shit, my stomach sinks at the thought, and my gut tells me it's true.

How do you tell a person you just fucked all your life secrets? What does she really owe me? Not a goddamn thing.

I've been really unfair to her and couldn't see past my own bullshit. Usually, I am the man at your back, but I left her alone for months. Given her background, I could have done some real damage between us. I never even opened my eyes past my own doubts to see it. I never gave her myself in order to build her up.

I am going to team build the fuck out of her until I have a really good reason not to be on her team anymore.

New plan, new day, no more excuses and no more running for either of us. I'm getting behind these girls.

I have to hold my chuckle in because now is not the time to tell them a pun.

Starting over, I clear my mind and throat. I am going to support these chicks and be their hero, and I'm going to make their demons fucking pay for fucking with my bitches.

And... I am back to where I was before.

Kat

Tami and I made dinner together tonight. It's nice to have company even though we have a hard time telling each other about our pasts. Both of us still carry our own problems, but it works because we respect each other's space. Maybe one day I can trust people again, but I don't know when. Tami makes it easier to want to try.

She places a salad and spaghetti on her plate, and I do the same. Together, we sit on the couch to watch some garbage reality T.V. I just like hearing her laugh. I hate the show, but I suffer through the drama because I think she missed that part growing up.

The front door swings open and I choke on the noodles I just shoved into my mouth. My heart hammers in my chest before that big stupid asshole barges in. Tank.

Noodles are sticking out and I choke on whatever managed to slide down my throat. It must be really classy looking with food halfway in and out of my mouth and choking while fighting to stay alive and breathing.

"Hello, ladies!"

He slams the door shut and then notices my dilemma of dying. I bend over my plate and cough my food back out. Saliva drips uncontrollably with it. Tami gets up to help me, handing me a napkin and gently rubbing my back. If I wasn't about to die, her touch would freak me out.

Tank runs over, standing in front of me with concerned puppy eyes. "Sorry, beautiful, I didn't mean to scare you. It is hard to look at something so pretty and not get all choked up, babe, but don't kill yourself over me." His hands move to cover my mouth from spewing hateful words back, like, *get the fuck out* and *why are you here?!*

"Not in front of the kid. Let's have a nice dinner, yeah?"

He doesn't wait for me to respond but helps himself into the kitchen and walks out humming to himself and commenting, "I'm starving, K-love." When he says 'starving' his eyes roam up and down my body.

Tami giggles at his theatrics and sits over in the La-Z-Boy, leaving the only available spot next to me on the couch, the little traitor. Tank sits down and tugs me along to sit right next to him. I swallow the large golf ball lodged in my throat. The alien feeling of something so normal feels so foreign that it's just wrong.

Tank takes a forkful of food and slurps up the noodles. My eyes blink because words are just beyond me in this moment. He eats the salad and his French bread without any added sound effects. What's his freaking deal?

Tami looks over to me and then Tank, bugging her eyes out saying, '*Do you hear this?*' I reply with my eyes, '*Loud and clear, I'm sitting right next to him!*'

The distress builds and I can no longer hear the T.V., but only the large sucking noise coming from next to me. About the fifth bite into his spaghetti, I lose all my self-control from the obnoxious noise.

Reaching into my side holster, I rip out my gun and point it at his face. "What the fuck is wrong with you?" I growl. "Make one more noise and I swear—"

Before the rest of the words can leave my mouth, Tank has a hand around the gun, then reaches up, twisting and taking it from my hand right before it goes off into the ceiling. I look up and there lays a bullet whole.

"You didn't even have that on safety when you pointed it at my face, Kat!" Tank booms at me. "There is something seriously fucking wrong with you, woman."

A lesser woman might've cowered at the scary angry biker man. But not me, no. I bust out laughing like I haven't done in years. Years of pent up loneliness creeps out uncontrollably with each hysterical, therapeutic release. His honesty should be hurtful, but it is true.

Tank's face relaxes and laughs with me after informing me, "You will never get your security deposit back for that, and I'm not fixing it for you either."

He picks up his plate and finishes eating, minus the loud slurping, making a point to show me his smaller bites before shoving his fork into his mouth. My face relaxes, and I smile at the big dumbass.

Tami watches us with little hearts in her eyes which makes me hope that a piece of me isn't broken after all. If she can see it, can it be real? Can Tank be real?

He jokes around with her and gets caught up in the drama of the show with her. It makes me feel good that she has someone not so ice cold who can relate to her.

He makes me feel so good and so alive that it scares me. If Matias, my husband, could almost destroy me, what could Tank do to me?

Another few hours pass while we're T.V. binging before Tami politely excuses herself, quietly standing up. Like a real sweetheart, Tank stands and gives her a hug goodnight.

"You doing okay, baby T? If there is anything you need, you come and talk to me, the big T. I will take care of it."

Tami dies of laughter, a sound she doesn't even make while watching this garbage, a sound of pure happiness. "Is this like I'm the little spoon and you're the big T-spoon?" she giggles again.

"Yep, I'm your big brother, T-spoon. You come talk to me every once in a while, and check in, yeah?"

Tami dives for him and wraps her arms around him. She doesn't let go for a minute, soaking him in. Tank naturally comforts and supports her, then pats her back and tells her, "Off to bed with you, lil' T."

She does just that, scampering off with light feet and a light heart. I want to be her so badly.

Tank dives back into the couch, scratching the floor with his weight. My eyes dart around the room, not sure how to navigate this now that we're alone. I've never been in a situation like this, ever.

"How was your day, Kit Kat? You shoot anyone, or *try* to shoot anyone, other than me?" I shake my head *no*, and he bats his eyelashes, "Good, that means you really love the Road Dog then, and only him."

I shake my head again but push him away, or I try to move the hulking man, shaking my head again. "Only you, Tank, can drive me bat shit crazy enough to do that."

"Kat," his voice drops serious. "I'm here for you too, when you are ready to trust me. I hope you tell me everything someday."

His hand comes up and touches my face. "I'm sorry I've been gone and away." He leans forward and kisses my lips so softly, I don't even move.

My chest constricts with the gentle pain he's inflicting on me. His strong fingers graze over my cheeks before he kisses me again. "Go to bed, baby, it's late. I'm sleeping on the couch, unless you have a guest bedroom?"

I look at him, confused as to why he would be sleeping here.

"I'm not leaving you unprotected, you need me."

The stubborn side of me wants to fight, to yell and scream. I get up from the couch and lead him to the other spare room that we have, then leave to go to my room, feeling so unsure of myself. Then there is the side that allows him, for now, to watch my back.

I tell myself it's because of Tami, and I hope I'm right, that what I'm doing is the right thing, because I am so damn tired.

CHAPTER 29

Kat

We fall into an easy rhythm for the next few weeks. It's almost a normal, domestic setting when Tank comes over every night, and, sometimes, he even cooks for us.

Little by little, he and Tami break my walls down. I start laughing at the stupid shows that entertain them, and I comment here and there how stupid they are together.

I think I love Tank just a tiny bit because of his softness that I've never seen or felt in my life.

Watching him with Tami scares me because he is so different from me. I'm not sure that Tank knows of my level of involvement with the MC. I believe he suspects it, but I don't know that he knows the jobs I have helped with or actually do.

The dirty cop that ran Axl off the road, I lured him in for a few weeks with a few dates and the promise of sex before tying him up and letting Blade and Axl kill him.

Blade asked me after that to hunt down more information on Tony Riva, and I reported back what I found. Which just lead back to the Cartel. They want Battle Born dead. He asked me to stand in the shadows as an extra set of eyes while they were in the building with Tony. I held the guns because I was never patted down as long as I was on the arm of one of the VIP gamblers who I had lured in from the bar the week before.

Would Tank still want to be here if he knew of the things I did?

Tonight, we drove here together after we blew up the building where the fights were being held. We killed, I have no idea how many men, while he whispered sweet words into my ear during it. It's normal to us now, like we went to work together and came home to shower the day off.

Except, we don't fuck each other, and I think that has to do with me. Outside of those intense moments, I keep him at an arm's length.

Tami's little frustrated growl breaks me away from my thoughts. She and Tank sit on the floor and stare at the laptop he bought for her to finish high school with a GED. He tries to explain math to her, several times. She's frustrated and he's red in the face from the effort he puts into not yelling at her.

"Lil' T, I swear to God, algebra is not that hard, just follow the rules here." He takes out a piece of paper from her notebook, and scribbles down the rules. The very last one he writes says, *Please marry for money because I'm scared for you.*

"Tank! God! I didn't go to school much as a kid!" she huffs and hits his head with a small pillow.

"It is sound advice. His accountant will take care of the money for you."

"You're stupid." She ignores the dig and finishes her work.

After she's done, she gets up with her supplies and laptop. "Kat, can we go shopping tomorrow?"

"Sure, honey, what are we looking for?"

She looks at Tank and then at me. I look at her, and then at Tank, and back at her.

"I'm going to bed." Tank gets up and walks down the hallway, quietly closing the door to his room.

Tami looks around, then at her feet. "I don't know how or where to look to buy a bra. Will you go with me and help me, maybe nicer underwear?"

My heart stops. She asked *me* and not Vegas or Dana?

"Sure, let's go after breakfast before work." I work really hard to make my voice not squeak.

"Thanks." Tami lunges for me like she did for Tank, and wraps her slender arms around me.

This girl, she melts my heart, man, and I have important manly shit to deal with. She's making me soft.

She lets go of me and walks to her bedroom. Before she gets to close her door, Tank sticks his head out and laughs at her, "Who are you buying the sexy undies for, lil' T? Those pound puppies?" His boisterous lough echoes throughout the house.

"Kat! Where is your gun? I'm going to shoot this asshole!" she screeches and slams her door shut, trying to block her embarrassment and hide her red face.

He yells back, "Don't yell and curse at your elders!" and slams his door shut after her, manically laughing still at my little T. Poor girl.

Shaking my head, I lock the front door and turn off all the lights, then walk down the dark hallway. Out of nowhere, large hands grab and push me through the door to my room, pinning me up against the wall.

"K-love, are you going to buy some sexy undies to show me tomorrow?" Tank rasps into my ear. His hands travel up my body. "I've missed you, baby, missed your smell and touch." He grabs my face and lays a possessive kiss on my lips. "When you trust me, I'll be ready."

My nails scrape up his arms and I thread my fingers through his hair. "Do you trust me?" he asks me.

I don't answer and deepen the kiss. Tank groans into my mouth, his tongue fucking mine.

When I don't answer, he suddenly pulls away and walks back to his room, in the dark. Leaving me breathless and alone with my thoughts.

Do I trust Tank?

Shrugging off my clothes and thoughts, I lie down in my bed. I toss and turn for a few minutes, unable to get comfortable enough to sleep. It feels as if a rush of heat hit my vagina and Tank lit the fire, I'm that turned on.

Getting out of bed, I grab my vibrator and slide back into the silk sheets, sans panties. Slipping the vibrator under the covers, I push the button and nothing. What the hell? I push the button again and nothing.

"Fuck."

I pull it out, frustrated, like, *really* frustrated, and open it. The batteries are gone. How, or rather *who* would steal my fucking batteries from a dildo?

Rage consumes me. I know who the fuck would do something so cruel and stupid, and toss the dido aside.

Jolting out of bed, I throw my pajama shorts and a tank on and march into his room, busting down the door.

When I am hovering over his bed, he lies there with his hands behind his head and his feet crossed. Through the moonlight, I can see his eyes twinkle like the stars, with mischief.

"Yes? Can I service you?" He somehow keeps a monotone voice but cannot conceal his big toothy grin.

Bending over so we are nose-to-nose, I growl, "Did you steal my batteries?"

"The batteries for your personal shaver? No."

I grit my teeth. "You know WHAT batteries I'm referring to, Tank," I whisper, dark and dangerous.

He laughs in my face. "Fucking A, I totally forgot I stole those. Here they are." His hand glides past my thighs and tugs the nightstand drawer open where there's a new ten pack of the batteries I would need.

"Asshole." I grab the pack out of spite and storm back to my room, slamming both doors. The sound of his laughter is loud enough to be heard over the noise I make on my way there.

I'm back in the same place I was before, sexually frustrated and now pissed off. How am I ever going to get to sleep?

After a few more tosses and turns, I think, fuck it. I load those batteries and flip my vibrator on and think of Tank the whole time while I get myself off.

He must hear the light buzzing go off because, as soon as I flip it off, he yells, "I'm happy I could be your hero, baby."

Fuck. My. Life.

The next day, I get a text from him. At least I think this is him because who else would do this?

Big Sexy Hero: Hey baby, club party tonight, have your ass here early.
Me: Why early, and what time is early?
Big Sexy Hero: IDK, how about five
Me: You don't know what time, do you?

Big Sexy Hero: I'll be your hero, baby, I'll take away your pain...
Me: Okay, fine, I'll be there "early." Shut up.

Pocketing my phone, I get back to work at the bar when an angry Jenn walks through the door.

Blade told us that she was back, but also warned us to give her some space until she was ready to be around people again. Jenn has come around more and more, and today she looks better, but still so angry.

Tank kept me in the loop with what was happening with her and asked if I could help her, the same with Cuervo.

The more time that passes, the more comfortable I feel around everyone.

It feels good to have Vegas in my corner. The day she found out I was her cousin, she was proud and excited to have me. Dana was surprised, but, blood or not, she too was welcoming. What scares me most is that one day this will all go away, and I'll be alone again. I know I will survive, but I don't want to do it alone.

As promised, the Prez and brothers met up with Cobra and killed him and his men. Even though Battle Born worked together to kill my dad, I couldn't care less. It's not a loss I felt because he was never in my life like a father should have been, and it's hard to forget that the asshole killed my mother. I had a drink, toasted on the day he died to a job well done. Another asshole down, a few more to go.

When Jenn sits down, I set a coke down in front of her and ask, "How are you holding up, Jenn?"

"Like hell has warmed over my soul, that's how I feel."

Her face is pale and the dark circles under her eyes show that. In fact, she's not living in this moment.

"I can help you with that kind of pain, Jenn."

Her eyebrows perk up in interest. "Do tell."

"I know where and how to find the man you want to kill most." I pause for a moment and take the money from the guy up at the front of the bar, trading him a draft beer. After he is gone, I continue, "I want that same thing that you do, revenge."

"I want torture, not just revenge." Her gaze lasers in on me, looking for any deceit here, but she won't find any.

"Jenn, I want that man dead, the one who hurt you, so that his brother can suffer the same hell."

"Cheers to death." Jenn holds up her coke and takes a drink.

I don't say much else to her for the rest of the afternoon. It doesn't look like she's ready to tell the whole story, but I have my suspicions of who it was that'd hurt her. If I'm right, it will fit in perfectly to take that bastard, Angel, out right before his brother.

After Emilia comes to relieve me from my shift at the bar, I head over to the clubhouse. Anxiety crawls at my skin from being here.

Walking inside, I see Tank and that he made us dinner. As I get closer, he pulls out a chair for me. "It's our date night. I didn't think you would be comfortable at a restaurant, so I made you... spaghetti." He pushes me toward the table.

He sits across from me and asks, "Beer or wine?" He smiles so big at me that it's blinding. Damn him, this is so sweet.

"A red wine would be great. Thank you."

Tank whistles loudly to Solo, "Bring my lady a red wine." Solo scowls over at him and he adds on, "A beer for me, too."

Solo brings our drinks. "I'm not a prospect anymore, dick." He places our drinks down and turns to leave us alone.

"But you are still the puppies in this pack," Tank hollers at Solo's retreating back. "He's so sensitive sometimes. You can only teach them so much, you know?" he comments and takes a large drink off his beer, chugging half of it in one go.

"Sure, Tank." I'm not even sure what he means, but I go along with it.

After we eat, he takes my hand and takes me on a tour around the MC. He shows me his garage, the MC garage, and I go with it. I tell myself it is more for recon, but really it is Tank. He makes the loneliness bearable.

When we reach the greenhouse, I'm actually very impressed by the pot that Pawn has growing out here and how well he is doing with it.

Tank then shows me every room in the clubhouse. Spider is a jerk and kicks us out with no interest in letting us hang out.

Together, hand in hand, we walk back outside to the picnic table out in the setting sun. He pulls me down to sit between his legs when he straddles the bench. My back to his front. He wraps me up in his arms and I close my eyes to the brightness of the sunset, resting my head back against his chest.

His nose runs up my neck and he places a few kisses along the way. "K-love, why did you get so many tattoos in the last few years? I think they are sexy as fuck, but they practically cover you."

I tense for a moment before he licks my skin and nips at my neck. He patiently waits for me, and I fight against the pride that has barricaded me for years. A wall of protection around me that kept me invisible from those who wanted to hurt me.

Tank squeezes me tighter. "Let me in, Kat. I will protect you like I do my brothers, you have my word."

Releasing a breath, I fight against my instincts. I float back in time and tell him what I can. It helps that he can't see my face, the window to it all.

"After I left Mexico, I hated the thought of his touch on me, that he had claimed any part of my body. I wanted to erase it all. Katherine Castillo died, the Black Widow was born. I haven't been called by that name in years. So, don't ever use it."

Tank traces over my skin, over the ink that tells the story of the woman who wears them. "Each one means something to you?"

"Yes, for every person I killed, for every woman or child they hurt. I took their pain and misery and killed the demon they wished they could. I replaced every feeling of despair with strength in every kill. To remember why I was still breathing. My purpose."

He holds me tighter, wrapping his arms around me. "To do what, love?"

"Kill my husband."

He kisses away a lone tear from my cheek, taking my pain and desperation instead of me taking from others.

"What about you, Tank? Did you have a love?"

"I thought I might have had one at one time, but no, I didn't."

"What happened?" The raw exposure of my earlier confession makes my voice crack.

"I was so young, like Solo and Pawn. I met this girl, Ava. Cute, young college kid. She loved riding on the back of my bike and on my dick at night. I was prospecting. The night of my patch-in party, she didn't show up."

He rests his chin on top of my head before finishing. "She ditched me because her real boyfriend had proposed. I was just a dirty secret on the side. Hurt like a motherfucker for a while."

"Then you got over her?"

"Well, you could say that."

"What does that mean?"

"I put enough bitches underneath me for a while that she became just another face."

"Jesus Christ, Tank." I can't help but cover my eyes. "You did not just tell me that!"

He whispers into my ear, "I only want *you* underneath me from now on, though."

He lets his hold around me go and helps me to turn around and face him. My hands roam through the thick hair on his head, then my nails drag through his short beard. Tank's eyes are a strikingly deep blue.

"You're light to my dark."

"You're my kinda dark, love."

CHAPTER 30

Tank

Life could not fucking be better, except that Cowboy invited the strippers out to the bonfire. A very pregnant Vegas and Dana don't look happy, and Kat turned into a possessed cat as soon as Topaz walked in. It has been months since our last run in, but apparently not enough time for Kat.

If I could, I would beat the shit out of Cowboy for ruining my date night. Epic retards, these guys.

The girls form an alliance on the other side of the fire, laughing and talking. I keep an eye on Kat and Topaz. I hope Topaz isn't stupid enough to approach the girls, but you never know.

"You talk your shit out with Kat?" Blade asks.

"Things are better, we'll see how it goes."

"What about her Ol' Man?" Axl questions, taking a chug out of his beer.

"Whatever it is that we have to do, we need to square it up. Soon," I look over to Blade.

"Aye, we need to get the word out to the other clubs and get Saint on board with getting Jenn together and ready."

When I look back over to the girls, I see that Kat is gone. I try not to look around for her. Where could she have gone anyway?

I shoot the shit with Axl about his bike for a few more minutes before hands touch my back. Honest to God, had I been able to see what was going to happen, I would have stopped it.

She reaches around my waist from behind, wrapping her arms around me. My arms go up a bit to give her access to my body. Except, this is where it all goes to shit.

Kat is standing in front of me and *not* behind me!

"Fuck," I look down and pull the woman leached onto me away, only to find it's Topaz. "Go," I bark at her and she scampers off with hurt feelings and slumped shoulders.

Kat is hauling ass across the back yard, too. I rub my hands over my face. "Why me?"

"Dude," Axl points his beer, "you have about thirty seconds to reach her before this goes nuclear and you get shot, this time for real. Run, go!"

I take off running to catch up to her and grip her arm to tug her back right before she reaches the door. She spins around with a vengeance and a fist. I block her hit and catch her knee to my nuts, thank fuck. I turn her around in my arms and pin her to the wall where the guys get a kick out of my distress.

"Calm down, Kit Kat!" my voice growls at her.

"*Pinche puta, chinga tu pinche madre, bastardo,* asshole!"

"What the fuck was *that*? Babe, I thought that was you."

"You lie, Tank," her voice gets thicker with her accent and it breaks just enough to where I can hear it.

"Don't hit me, shoot me or cut me, okay? I'm going to let you go, okay?" She doesn't answer me.

I back up just a bit, but, in the dark, I can't see her face except for the shadows of the fire that flicker across her face when I turn her around. Some deep-rooted pain flickers in her eyes, just like the flames.

I bend down and pick her up, cradling her to my chest. I take her to my room and shut the door behind us, then sit down with her in my lap.

"Kat, love, that was an accident. I wouldn't have let that happen if I didn't think that was you, babe. Only you."

Kat, the vulnerable woman inside who has been forgotten, looks up at me but won't speak the words that show her weakness. Has she ever been vulnerable in her life? I kiss her forehead, cheeks and lips.

"You know how to stop that from happening?"

She shakes her head no.

"You claim me as your man, and if you kick one girl's ass, they will all be scared to touch your man. Easy, babe, you can't pull guns though. Blade will flip his shit on you, and then on me."

Her eyes lighten and she shakes her head at me.

"You trust me?"

She bites her lip, "Yes, Tank, I trust you."

My hands grab her head at hearing her words, and my heart races with the blood pumping through my body as I'm wondering if that means what I think, or hope, that it means.

Kat

He asks the biggest question of all. Of course he wants to know. My heart breaks because I can't give him what I know he wants, not yet.

"In time, please give me time. Is that enough for now?"

He rolls me over to lie on top of me. "What's in your head, Kat?" He gently pushes the hair away from my face.

"A lot of regret, pain and revenge. He has to die, Tank, for me to stay alive. Or he will take away the thing that matters the most to me the world." My eyes flutter shut, not being able to answer beyond that.

"I'm going to be your hero, baby, I'm going to be the man that takes that darkness away and gives you what you want, to be free."

A knock at the door interrupts the bleak moment of sadness that I am anxious to escape from.

Escape from the prison that has become my life. Revenge.

Tank

"Prez wants you in church ASAP," Pawn yells through the door.

I kiss Kat on the forehead and push up from the bed while saying, "Head out to the bonfire with the girls, or stay in here, but, Kat, you better keep your ass on the premises."

I have to leave to take care of business. This is getting old. Every time I get anywhere with her, something comes up.

Doubt creeps into my heart like an old friend. Is she staying with me because her husband will kill her if she leaves here?

For now, I push the thoughts away and go to work. Blade is sitting at the table with a seething Spider and Cowboy. The door shuts behind us all and I open the discussion, "I better not be in here because of you two." I point a meaty finger at each of their chests.

Spider and Cowboy remain in their standoff, glaring at each other. Blade throws down the gavel and all heads turn to him. He points it at each of them, "Are you two going to fight over bitches? Go to blows over a woman neither of you have claimed? Spider, if Jazz is yours, then you need to claim her, or back off."

Spider's vicious look turns to Blade and Axl who is sitting next to him. "*Really*? I remember someone called dibs on Vegas, and," he looks over to Axl, "your princess."

I jump in and stop Spider from getting a knife in his chest for challenging the Prez and VP at the table. "Brother, if you laid your intentions out there, everyone should agree to back the fuck off." I pointily stare at Cowboy. "Aren't you fucking busy chasing Topaz's ass around anyway?"

"Not when she's hanging off of *you*," he spits at me.

"Oh, I get it now. You're being a little bitch and went to the next chick you could use to piss her off. Grow the fuck up, Cowboy. She is a fucking stripper, you stupid fuck, fuck her and move on." I take a calming breath. "We have a lot more important shit to worry about, not this fucked up grade school shit."

I turn my attention back to the Prez and VP. "When can we get Jenn on board to move forward?"

"So we can settle Kat's shit too for you?" Cowboy is pushing me like no other dumbass I've ever seen. I lunge forward and slam my fist into his nose. Blood spurts and spatters from the impact. More than likely, the nose is broken.

"I was patient with you, motherfucker, and you kept running your mouth. You need a fucking time out, sit down."

Pawn tosses him a smirk like, *Yeah, bitch, be humble.*

I take my seat next to Blade, the anger trying to consume me into pounding out my frustrations some more on Cowboy. Axl looks amused and we'll high-five later. Blade clears his throat, trying to get back to business, but I know he wants to laugh too.

"Saint, is Jenn ready to come forward? I don't want to put pressure on her. But this does need to be done."

Saint looks up, "I think I can get her to come in. Give me a day or two?"

Blade nods his agreement and stares at the room. "Get the fuck out." He slams the gavel down and the men leave to head back out to the bonfire.

"Tank," Blade calls for me to stay when everyone in the room has left and the door shuts. "What have you found out?"

It pisses me off that he asks. However, I get it. His loyalty is to the club and not to Kat.

"Her name is Katherine Castillo, married to the Cartel boss. She's protecting something, a family in

California. I haven't made the connection to her yet. Spider is helping me."

"Did she tell you that her husband has been the puppet master behind all of this? The war, the transport, Johnny, the diamonds, everything. He wants the northern rights, and was going through her father, Cobra, as the middleman."

I sit there and let it sink in. It doesn't surprise me, but, at the same time, it does. It's just another war, but, this time, against the Cartel.

"It's time we call the chapters in."

I just hope that, by the end of this, we all survive and there is a club still standing, regardless of Kat, me or the brothers.

The Cartel has been playing us for a long time and wants what is ours.

They will want us all dead for taking her.

Some wars must be won by sacrificing the Queen.

CHAPTER 31

Tank

After last night's call to all the chapter Presidents, they are on their way to Reno to have a meeting, as a whole club, with Jenn. Also, the bosses want to go over the plan with Kat. That, no one knows the full details of it just yet.

I'm worried where that leaves Kat, and then us. I know that I can't run from this, that we have to face what is coming at us. It still scares the shit out of me though.

I park outside of The Black Rose and go in search of Kat. I don't give a fuck what she has going on, I need her. Crave to feel her and be with her. This decoy job for her is going to have to be put on hold.

Inside the bar, I charge forward to where she's standing, serving drinks, and plenty of guys are gathered to get a glimpse of those fat tits behind the bar.

"Tami," I call out. "Call in to Vegas and let her know that Kat has gone home sick." Tami smiles and pulls out her phone to do as I asked. Smart kid.

Kat stands there stunned as she's handing over a row of shots to one of the waitresses. Once the tray is out of the way, I pull her to my side and escort her out of the bar. As soon as we reach my bike, I hand her a helmet and jump on. She slides on behind me, not an inch between us.

I weave us through the heavy traffic until we reach the mountains. It starts to thin out and I take her to a secluded cabin. When we're parked, she jumps off and looks around the small property.

"What is this place?" Kat smiles at the sun that creeps through the trees and the shadows that flicker around from the clouds.

"This is our place, one where no one else has been. When you want to run, Kat, I want you to come here. It is your safe place with me. Promise me that you will always meet me here if we are ever separated or when you are scared."

I step closer, and the leaves on the ground crunch under the weight of my boots.

Kat looks up at me. "Not a person knows about this place besides you and me?"

"Not a soul, K-Love, it's ours."

Something finally breaks through to her and she takes one step and then two more until she's standing right in front of me. The woman that I've always pictured her to be looks free, at least in this moment, at least with me.

"Will you touch me, Tank? I've missed you so much. Only true love can hurt like this. You have ruined me. I can't live or love in a life without you."

Her hand reaches out and tugs me to her by pulling on my cut.

My hands reach under her ass and I pick her up. Her legs wrap around my waist and her mouth caresses mine with a gentle touch of her lips, her tongue snaking out to wrap around mine. My fingers tighten around her and squeeze her ass.

Her reaction to me is so pure that it erases any doubt.

She belongs with me.

I walk us through the front door and shut it with a kick of my boot. She pushes my cut off and I hear it hitting the floor, shortly followed by her shirt and bra that she removes by breaking from our kiss. My hands grip her waist and I easily toss her onto the bed. She bounces on the thick mattress and I chase after her, pushing her to lie down on her back.

I pull her boots and black jeans off, leaving her in a red thong. She brings her legs up and exposes her pussy to me through the lace. It's sexy as fuck. Something silver catches my eyes and I blink.

"I pierced my clit, Tank." She takes a hold of her thong, pulling at the lace between her pussy lips and exposing a little more of the bar that runs through her clit.

"Fucking hot, babe, pull those panties off." My voice is labored from the lust laced through my veins, hitting my dick. I kick off my boots and pull out a condom from my pocket before pushing my jeans and boxers down, then kicking those away too.

"Touch your pussy, K-Love, get yourself ready for me."

She lifts her ass just enough to glide the lace down and toss it aside before opening her legs wide for me. A finger traces down the inside of her thigh before it reaches her pussy and gently spreads her lips for me. Two of her fingers glide in and out a few times before taking them to her clit and smoothly spreading her lust for me.

"Several times I touched myself while thinking of your big dick." She pants, and, on auto pilot, my hand tugs at my dick, stroking myself as I'm watching my queen light herself up for me.

"I would come alone, moaning your name," her voice catches, "I almost came on the ride up here from the vibrations on your bike. I wanted to rub myself all over you."

"Fuck, baby, don't stop rubbing your clit. Rub it harder, faster, I want to watch you come."

I keep a slow pace but a firm grip, not wanting this to end for me yet.

She moans and arches into her own touch.

"I have dreams of you, of our night in Vegas and wake up to my body coming just from your memory."

She pulls her legs back even further, almost begging me to thrust inside of her. She exhales on a long moan, and I can see her pussy contract from her release.

My body reacts like a beacon to hers, and I fall to my knees before her, on the floor. My hands graze the outside of her thighs, then I place kisses on the inside of each one.

"You're beautiful, K-Love, and all mine." I place one kiss on her sensitive pussy and ask, "Kat, baby, I know you are married, but I need to know that you'll be my Ol' Lady, that's all I need."

I take her fingers that stroked her pussy into my mouth and take back from her what is mine.

"Yes," she hiccups out.

I dip my head and take a long lick of her, then play with her clit, soft and slow. She builds up quickly and chants my name, her hands clawing at the sheets. Her hips start bucking into my face and a hand reaches out to grab a hold of my hair. I let her take control and ride my face.

"Sh-i-t!" She calls out and comes, holding on to me a moment longer as I lick her back down. She releases the tight lock hold she has on my head and I push us both up the bed, with me lying between her legs.

My body rocks into her and I coat my dick with her release. My teeth nip at the skin on her neck. The salty taste invades her sweet flavor that's still on my tongue.

"I won't break any part of you, Kat, and, one day, you will believe that with your whole heart." I rest my hand gently between her breasts. "I'm going to love you softly and fiercely until the day you die, I promise you this."

And I *will* keep my promise until I die. A tear leaks from the corner of her eye and I kiss it away. "Don't cry, I love you," I rasp.

Kat opens her glossy eyes to me, and I see that they're filled with tears. My thumbs wipe them away.

"I will be your hero, the man that will fall for you every day and fight all your demons." She shakes her head at me, but I hold her still. "I see the pain and ghosts in your eyes, the ones that crushed your heart." I let out a deep sigh. "I will also be the man to make that heart beat again."

She sobs and whispers into the silence, "I love you, too, Tank, don't break me."

"Never, K-Love." Fuck the condom and fuck tomorrow. I plunge into her body, impaling my dick into her velvety soft pussy. I'm claiming my woman. It doesn't matter what tomorrow brings.

Soft and slow, I enjoy the feel of us connecting as I'm sliding in and out of her. I can't get enough of it and her. I've never experienced the feeling of being bare inside of a woman.

My hand holds Kat in place by her hip as I grind my pelvis against hers and her clit. She moans with me and we pick up the pace, thrusting and grinding.

"Come with me, baby, soak me," I beg her because it's been a while, and this feeling of us together bare is lighting me up and taking me to places I have never been. A few more pumps and she lets go with another orgasm, squeezing the shit out of my dick. I still when my dick shoots my release into her.

Kat. My woman. My Ol' Lady.

I collapse on top of her, catching my breath before rolling over and tucking her into my side.

"I'm buying you a diamond clit ring, Kat," I growl into her and lay a possessive hand over her pussy. "I'm going to marry you some day but I'm marking this as mine now."

She doesn't say anything, but her chest starts to shake with laughter. "Cat got your tongue?"

We clean up and look around the cabin a bit before we take off, heading back into town. I know in my gut what is coming tonight, and thank fuck that Kat and I are on the same page when we get back.

With Kat by my side, we walk into the Battle Born clubhouse. I don't miss the stares that we get from the patch holding members. I grin at all of them because, now, she is untouchable; she is mine and under the entire club's protection.

Together we walk into the meeting room for Church where Saint and Jenn should be coming in soon. I greet the out of town chapter members and introduce Kat. She shakes each of their hands and doesn't flinch at some of the glares she receives from them.

Jenn hesitantly walks in with Saint at her back. The men all stand to show her great respect and tell her just that. Stryker picks her up in a great bear hug, having helped raised her himself. Even Ice, the coldest motherfucker here, supports her by wrapping an arm around her and saying, "You have my help also, Jenn. Let me know who to kill first, and it's done, princess."

All the members squeeze in along with Vegas and Dana who have settled in next to Blade and Axl for this meeting.

Jenn breaks her silence and tells the room the shit hand she was dealt and apologizes for her actions afterward. Which none of us, not a single one, was expecting.

She used pills and booze to try and wipe the memories from her rape away. It was nothing we couldn't handle and was nothing she should've apologized for, regardless of what she had said or done before.

Jenn's face pinches with worry and pain. "I'm sorry you had to see that and I'm sorry for the pain I caused because of it. You see, when you live in the dark, the lies become your truth. A prison I didn't want to escape. I'm better now."

She continues on, telling us the details of her rape and who did it.

Kat's body tightens next to me and I can feel that she knows exactly who the man is that raped Jenn.

"The day I was raped, the man, Angel, he said a few things that I think you need to know about. He knew who my father was but didn't realize that I didn't know. He had been expecting me to be sold as his bride, but, I believe Kat took my place."

Jenn stops and looks apologetically over to us. "It wasn't until recently that I learned that Kat was my cousin. Coincidence that she showed up shortly after?"

Jenn pauses for a moment, not letting her eyes leave Kat. "I'm not the only one who's had to hide behind their lies to survive. I'm guessing that you took my spot and escaped, and they were looking for you when Angel found and raped me."

Kat's eyes show all the anger that she normally guards so closely. "That would be the brother of Angel, Matias. Also known to his people as '*the gift of god*'. He is the boss of the Mexican Cartel. You are right. My father had decided that I was more of a powerful trade than you. You were forgotten, but not to Angel, it seems. When the club war broke out, I escaped and started plotting my own revenge. Men were scattered, and I wouldn't be surprised if the others don't know what Angel did. The things you said were very personal. He believes you are his. If you don't kill him, he *will* rape you again, and, more than likely, has been enjoying your pain from afar."

My hand squeezes Kat's, I think more for myself than for Kat, because she lived with that monster, she was married to the devil and survived. I don't know that I will ever be able to hear the words of the torture she lived through.

The meeting is over shortly after that and the room files out. I know that this is just the first meeting before the real one.

Kat and I stay with the rest of the seat holding members. Half look at her with pity and the other half with anger.

Stryker in particular is looking intently at her. "Every word I have heard, is it true what you are saying? No lies?" he raises a brow. "That the Cartel orchestrated this mess that's been going on for years? You have one shot with me and one only."

Kat lets go of my hand and pulls out a thumb drive from the lining in her bra. She reaches up under her armpit and pushes it out before passing it over.

Ice smiles, a wicked gleam catching in his eye at the small show of Kat's flesh that was exposed.

Holding the memory stick in her hand, she states, "This has information Matias collected for years while I lived with him, information on you and Cobra. It will show you how he manipulated you both to get what he wanted. For years after I left, I watched him and tracked what I could of what I could find for you."

Kat holds out the thumb drive. "This is my life and death, and the only thing this will prove is that it would benefit us both to kill him."

Stryker takes it from her. "Don't go far and don't try and run from me," he warns her, truly looking and sounding like the strongest President on the west coast that he is, with full weight behind his threat.

I step forward and place a hand on Kat's shoulder, standing by her side. "She's my Ol' Lady, and I back her a hundred and ten percent."

Blade's face goes from relaxed to pissed in seconds, a beating I'm sure to take for not telling him beforehand. Stryker looks at him, then his eyes like lasers examine Kat from head to toe. "Vest and brand?"

"She will wear it and soon," I confirm without any hesitation or fear. Kit Kat on the other hand may freak the hell out as soon as we get out of here.

I know for a fact that she has no guns on her, so at least I know that I have a chance to survive.

"You both head out tomorrow to Mexico. Get your shit settled," Stryker warns and the Prez of the mother chapter walks out.

Blade holds his anger back not to cause a scene but I'll fucking pay for this later.

Hot on Kat's heels, I charge out to keep up with her since she stormed out after Stryker did.

Kat

"What the fuck was that, Tank?"

My hands blast the front door wide open and it flies, ricocheting off the wall as I'm stomping down the stairs with Tank on my tail.

I stop abruptly and point a finger to his face, about to spit my scorn at him, but he stops me with my mouth open.

He shrugs off my angry tirade, smacks my hand out of his face, then paces out to his bike that is parked out in front of the building. I follow him this time, wanting to rip into him.

"You agreed, didn't you, Kat, to be my woman not hours ago? Let's get one thing straight between you and me." Tank takes one large step forward, towering over me and crowding my space, pushing me back a few steps.

"I call the fucking shots when it comes to my club and you. I saw where they were going to go. I made the choice to give you my protection and I'm not going to discuss club business with you." He stands firm with a wide stance and arms crossed over his chest.

Taking one step back, I glare at his face. "I'm no man's fucking puppet." I spit the harsh words like venom at him. "You get on board with that shit. When it comes between you and me, we will agree or there will be nothing to agree on," my voice raises with frustration. "I'm not putting shit on my body until I'm fucking ready, Tank, so fuck your manly shit. I can take care of myself."

"Fucking laughable when you are here for the club's help, Kat. You can't take down that asshole alone. And you need to learn to trust me, I did that for *you*. Can you get that through your head? Do you understand the beat down I'm gonna take from Blade for doing that?"

"I hate the fucking games, Tank. It's hard as hell for me to trust people. All my life I have been nothing but a pawn, and when I see shit like that going down without a heads up, it makes me feel like you took me to the mountains and fucked me only to get what you wanted."

Tank laughs out loud and swings his muscled arms wide. "No shit, Kat. I fucked you and told you I loved your crazy ass and asked you to be my Ol' Lady. I asked *you* before I announced it to the club. Chill the fuck out. You're making shit bigger in your head than it is, woman."

Pain, fear and anger overcome my senses, and, before I know what I'm doing, I've raised my hand, aiming it for Tank's face. He doesn't flinch from my reaction but, at the last second, captures my wrist before my hand strikes him. With a firm grip, he holds my wrist captive for a moment and glowers into my eyes.

I hate that the emotions come out when he's around. *He* is my weakness and my undoing, and, when he is gone, I fear that I would die without him.

I try to tug my arm back from his iron grip. He holds tight and observes me, my wild and crazy heart on display, and it fucking hurts.

"Let me go," I demand through clenched teeth.

"No, K-Love. I will not let you go." Tank lowers my wrist and tugs my body into his. I fall against his chest. His strong commanding arms wrap around my body and he holds me tight.

"Don't ever try and hit me again." His deep soothing baritone wraps around me. "Don't try and shoot or stab my ass. You've got some issues, love. But that abusive shit has got to stop. I'm never going to lay a hand on you or hurt you out of anger." Patient and strong loving hands slide up and down my back.

Love. He has shown me love and protection and I threw it into his face. I break in the front yard and crumble down every wall of defense I had against this man. Deep, gut wrenching sobs break free like a dam of a lifetime, flooded with betrayal and lies.

My life has been so diseased with it that everyone is a target and there is no truth anymore.

Tank wraps me up and carries me to the garage, kicking every man in there out. He sits with me in a chair until the pain subsides and the tears have dried.

"I'll be the man who protects you, even from yourself."

CHAPTER 32

Kat

Tank held me through the night after we took a long ride home together, on his bike. Probably so I could cool off, but also because he knew we needed it. To be together without all the drama, and live free. Even if it was for only a few moments, it was needed.

He didn't say a word when we got into bed, but he let me wrap myself up in him. There are parts of me that need to heal, but, at least for now, he gave me him, his strong support.

These small things he does are so different than what I am used to. I'm thankful he gives me the space and silence to adjust to them.

Overnight, I soaked him in, and I was ready to battle again. I packed our stuff for the long journey ahead. We left the very next morning, after the interrogation from the club, heading to Mexico.

I get why his brothers would doubt me and I can't fault them for it one bit. Tank and I had a huge fight because I refused to get his brand, not while his club doubted me. It's for their protection.

I know that it would make Tank feel better, but that's too fucking bad. I haven't worked my ass off to become the Black Widow to pussy out and roll over the easy way. I'll wear his brand when I'm good and fucking ready to. When the time is right. I fucking love the man, but it is important for the club to trust me too.

Getting Jenn and I over the boarder was a piece of cake. I met the Hoffmans' friends during my stay there. Luckily, the man had served time in the military and recognized our situation, gracefully looking away. He said that he would help as long as I contributed to the mission. I gave him a stack of cash for those kids in Mexico City, and I have no doubt he used that money for them. I'm no fool either. I saw the redemption in his eyes. He felt that this was his penance. To each their own.

Once we were there in Mexico City, it was easy to track Korina, my sister, down. She never strayed far from the Cartel, and she was much easier to find than them. I knew she hadn't died on the day I left. I think a part of me kept her alive because I hadn't been ready to kill her at the time. But, once I faced her again, I was. I put a bullet in her and her lover, Esteban, with no regret. After all, they did keep me from my happiness and my child.

Even though killing Korina had to be done, it felt like a stake had been run through my heart. I mourned the loss of my twin sister. Not the shell she had become, but the sister I had had as a child. I had to say goodbye to her, and a piece of me held on to that. Korina would have come back to kill me or someone that I loved.

We were down there for about a week before the mission to Mexico was done, and, thank God that every single one of us came back alive. And the best part, *Jenn* is alive and present with her soul in this world. I think she can finally move forward, and I am content that she can.

This jaded game is getting old, and it feels like none of us are winning. When does it stop? When we all die from our choices?

Even now that we've been back for a while, Tank is giving me time to feel my way through the darkness, and process the events. Others may see me as cold or heartless. What they don't see is a heart that has been abused and that I do what I can to live to fight another day. Fighting for a future where lies and deceit don't live.

I will do whatever it takes to get there. I will kill anyone for that, to escape the betrayal and imprisonment.

Old habits die hard though and even more so now that I'm getting so close to the end of my own personal mission, killing Matias. I look even harder for signs of him. The closer you get to the fire, the hotter it gets.

I begged Spider and Blade to act faster and move in on Matias while we had the advantage. Unfortunately, they didn't agree, and that leads me to now, about nine months out from when we left Mexico. Waiting for him to make an appearance.

We've discussed strategies and made some tentative plans. Their choice is to draw Matias out, take him out of his comfort zone. To bring him here. And that makes me nervous. However, I trust them to make this work.

It hurt like a son of a bitch to go back to Mexico, and was a gamble if I would make it back alive. Just knowing that I wasn't alone for a change and had Tank and Jenn with me made it possible. That chokes me up, because the truth hurts.

I pray that they don't abandon me with the next phase of our plan.

CHAPTER 33

Kat

A lot of things have happened since I've joined forces with the Battle Born brothers, and I think over my time here in the last year or so. How much I have grown.

When Vegas and Dana had their babies, Tank held on to me through the torturous moments I held their precious children. I had to force myself not wishing to die from the pain of holding them in my arms.

I needed to take my mind off things for a bit. So, as a surprise, Tank and I took Tami out one day, and we found her an apartment to live in on her own. We called it a graduation gift, from earning her diploma online.

It made me chuckle when Tank said, "Woman, we do everything ass backwards, but look at our little T-spoon, all grown up and in her own house. We did that, K-Love."

It was perfect timing too because she needed her independence as a woman, and I also needed her to get away from me. I couldn't live with myself if I lost her in the crossfire. I've greatly enjoyed watching her grow even more while living on her own.

Since the pound puppies, Solo and Pawn, both went after Tami, finally, I have been a little more relaxed. There may have been a few times along the way when I planted the idea in everyone's head to get the ball moving.

Vegas and Dana, along with Tank, jumped at the idea of meddling and helping her out. I did it out of love for Tami. They obviously love her too and I need her protected.

Even though Solo came out as the victor and stole her away, Pawn will get his happily ever. I will see to it.

Do you believe in fate or that the road carries in the direction meant to be traveled? I do, I believe in rolling with it and having faith.

Even when it feels like you are crumbling, don't. Faith and a set of brass balls will see you through.

Once Pawn learns faith and earns those brass balls, he will find out the rest of his story. Because he will be ready to fight for it. I feel it in my gut, and I pray that I will be around to meddle in it.

All shit broke loose with killing that crooked cop, and his fiancé sought out her revenge that landed Pawn in prison. She framed him for beating the hell out of another man and planting drugs on Pawn. Feather set him up for what we did, and the game of revenge continues.

Blade, Axl and I all feel responsible for how that shit turned out. Not a single one of us has uttered a word about what happened to him, but our guilt runs deep.

My heart clenched in agony on the day little Cash was born. Pawn was locked up and couldn't hold his son. It was a painful reminder of something that I understood better than anyone else on this earth.

Emily Scott, or Feather, died for her betrayal to the club. She was burned alive in a bonfire far out into the desert.

A wicked smile creeped up my face the harder she screamed, and, eventually, she stopped after a few minutes. What was left of Feather and her belongings was buried deep into the earth, never to be seen again.

Even through her death, the debt owed to Pawn would never be fully repaid because some things just couldn't be brought back, and that was time.

Time that is stolen is time lost forever.

However, Emily Scott will still be alive, on paper anyway.

My contacts couldn't get a location on Matias recently, and my anxiety runs rampant. Tank said to trust him and the club, and I have been doing that.

I completely and one hundred percent don't agree with their decisions, but I can't make them move any faster either.

I start making rounds, keeping an eye on everyone and everything daily. At the moment, I'm up on a hill, checking things out, when my heart sinks at what I see.

Tami parks and gets out of her car, then grabs Cash in his car seat from the back seat before coming back out to get his diaper bag. Seconds later, a black SUV pulls in at the curb and lifts the hood. The slick looking man walks up to her.

Tami, goddamn it, talks to him. My hands shake with fear of what he will do to her and Cash. I pull out my phone sending a quick text to let Spider know that Matias is here, with a simple "M."

Steeling my nerves, I dial the devil, his number forever imprinted in memory.

"Katherine," he stalls because he knows it's me. "Excuse me for a moment," I hear him explaining to Tami as he walks away from her. "*Mi amor*, time to come home to your *esposo*, yes?"

There is a real chance that I will die young, like I always thought I would, and die before I even get across the border. When he sees my skin and the tattoos that cover my once perfect complexion, he will be disgusted with my disobedience.

"Leave her alone and I will come home now."

"No games, or I kill them both." He waits for me to answer, and, when I don't, he promises, "Then, I will have my men shoot the other women and children next. If you tip her off."

"Let her go into the house and I'll walk over there now." I'm shaking because Matias could kill her out of spite. But if he does hurt her or Cash, I will run, and he knows it.

"Hello." He grabs Tami's attention and saunters back toward her. "I think it is just a loose hose. Thank you so much for coming out, but my mechanic just called me back."

"Oh, okay then, if you need some help, let me know," I hear her sweet voice responding.

Jesus, Tami, *just go into the house,* I want to yell at her.

Matias holds the phone at his side, and I begin to walk the last stretch of my freedom back to him. Pausing at the side of the house, I take out the drug I've had on me since my last conversation with Spider and Blade, and swallow the bitter pill, and the reality.

When Tami is safely inside, I step out from around the neighbor's house. Matias turns in my direction and fury replaces the mask that he wore for her. I hold my gun close to my side.

"As soon as both you and I are in the car, I will hand over the gun."

Matias grips my jacket and pulls me to him, wrapping his arms around me. An embrace that would look like a lover's hold. His teeth bite into my ear. "What have you done?" he snarls, and the demon comes out.

"What I had to."

"You will regret killing Korina and Esteban, and you will tell me where you've been hiding everything that is mine."

Before I can answer, Matias smashes his lips to mine.

I don't move. I freeze because there is no choice but to give in and save all their lives.

Matias bites my upper lip and pulls away before pushing me into the truck. Tami's confused face comes into view from her window right before the door is shut.

Raising the gun to shoot him, I fail before I can pull the trigger and I black out when a fist smashes my temple.

CHAPTER 34

Tank

"And?" These boys need more help then I swear I have time for. Freaking Cowboy thinks he can win a bet against me, the king.

My phone vibrates from a call and I hold up a finger before answering, "What's up, little T?"

She chokes on a sob and crying comes over the line. The blood in my veins instantly freezes and my heart stops.

"What happened, Tami? I need you to take some deep breaths and tell me everything."

Through hiccupping and hysterics, I hear everything that I need to know. Kat left me. For her *husband*.

She ran out on *us*.

There was never an us.

Once again, I was just the stupid biker that she wanted to fuck and use.

Fuck, how could I be so stupid?

"Thanks, T, I will figure out what is happening, okay?" At least I have enough in me to sell it to the kid that everything is okay. I hang up my call with Tami and throw my beer across the garage, shattering the glass in a million pieces.

A roar of bikes light up the driveway and I run out to see Axl, Blade and Spider jump on. Cowboy and I are hot on their tails, only just behind them.

We race down the freeway, after what, I don't know. I'm so high from the adrenaline that my blood pressure is the only thing that I can hear in my head.

We come up behind a black SUV and my heart stops cold. Is this the ride that Kat jumped into? Blade darts ahead and then Spider swerves in front of the car. They stomp on their breaks, almost crashing into the SUV. Not having another choice, the vehicle veers off the freeway and takes a side road.

Luckily, Cowboy and I are behind and are able to follow it. Pain and fury at her choice has me uncontrolled of my thoughts. Pulling out my gun, I aim and shoot at the tires. As I hit one, the vehicle swerves and takes a sharp right, barely making it around the corner.

Cowboy and I skid to a stop and turn back around. By the time we find the truck, it's empty and everyone has fled.

I look around for the direction that they could have run, but with the several surrounding buildings, there is no telling which way they went.

"Tank," Cowboy calls, but I can't move.

"Tank!" He screams this time and I turn toward him where he drags out of the backseat a lifeless Kat, bleeding from her head. "She's not breathing!"

Blade, Spider and Axl come up the road with a roar and take in the scene while parking their bikes, then run over to us. Like in slow motion, I paw at them to get to her.

Blade and Axl pull me back, yelling at me to calm down. But I can't. I don't know if I'm screaming her name or not. The confusion and shock cloud my senses and actions.

Spider takes her from Cowboy while giving him orders, and caries her off the street and into a building.

My mind snaps and I start punching at Blade and Axl. They fall back and I run for Kat, screaming her name when I get into the building.

"Tank, brother, she is gone. Stop making a scene and help me hide her before the cops get here." I hear sirens blasting into the distance.

My life dies on the day my K-Love becomes a dark angel in heaven. She finally escaped the pain and torture of her past.

Kat is the Queen we sacrificed to win the war.

Then why does it feel like I lost?

To Be Continued...

Fighting for Forever (Battle Born MC, Book 6)

Tank is shattered.

He lost the woman he loves and faith in his own MC. Together, they schemed behind his back and hid the truth from him. Even when all Kat's secrets are revealed, he wrestles with forgiveness and wonders if he will ever be able to trust her again.

The Black Widow.

That's the title Kat earned as she killed to survive after fleeing Mexico. Be that as it may, if she wants the MC's help to bringing down the cartel her only choice is to overcome her distrust in men.

Can Kat learn to let go and trust her feelings for Tank? Or will the past she can't escape destroy her and the MC?

TO THE READERS

Some roads, stories and choices change our lives forever. We never really know what tomorrow will be, only that faith in ourselves will make it okay in the end. We all struggle. I hope that you find some deeper meaning to these women in these books. That you see their strength, and some of that sticks to you.

This book, and the next, is for you. After I started Tank & Kat's book, it felt wrong to the series as a whole to cram it all into one book. It felt right to give them their whole story in two books. I hope, for those who wanted one book, that you forgive me and enjoy the story. This is my faith, truth and the road I chose and the story to tell.

Leave nothing left unsaid and regret nothing,

Scarlett

ABOUT THE AUTHOR

Scarlett Black is the author of the Battle Born MC Series. Not really knowing where a story will take her is what she loves most about writing. She strives to write about strong women and the men who love them. She believes in love and the miracles that come from it. She enjoys giving her fans a happily ever after worth melting their hearts. These may be books, but they are written with her heart and soul. She is Battle Born. Are you?

www.authorscarlettblack.com

Made in the USA
Monee, IL
30 October 2020

46407844R00157